Miracle

ALSO BY ELIZABETH SCOTT

Bloom

Perfect You

Living Dead Girl

Something, Maybe

The Unwritten Rule

Between Here and Forever

Miracle

ELIZABETH SCOTT

SIMON PULSE

NEW YORK LONDON TORONTO SYDNEY NEW DELHI

SIMON PULSE
An imprint of Simon & Schuster Children's Publishing Division
1230 Avenue of the Americas, New York, NY 10020
First Simon Pulse paperback edition July 2013
Copyright © 2012 by Elizabeth Spencer
All rights reserved, including the right of reproduction in whole or in part in any form.
SIMON PULSE and colophon are registered trademarks of Simon & Schuster, Inc.
Also available in a Simon Pulse hardcover edition.
For information about special discounts for bulk purchases, please contact
Simon & Schuster Special Sales at 1-866-506-1949 or business@simonandschuster.com.
The Simon & Schuster Speakers Bureau can bring authors to your live event.
For more information or to book an event contact the Simon & Schuster Speakers Bureau
at 1-866-248-3049 or visit our website at www.simonspeakers.com.
Designed by Angela Goddard
The text of this book was set in Adobe Caslon.
Manufactured in the United States of America
2 4 6 8 10 9 7 5 3 1
The Library of Congress has cataloged the hardcover edition as follows:
Scott, Elizabeth, 1972–
Miracle / by Elizabeth Scott. — 1st Simon Pulse hardcover ed.
p. cm.
Summary: Rising senior and star soccer player Megan Hathaway, unable to remember
the plane crash of which she was the sole survivor, feels like an empty shell and loses all
interest in her life and her friends, but unlikely friends help her face life as a "miracle."
ISBN 978-1-4424-1706-9 (hc)
[1. Survival—Fiction. 2. Aircraft accidents—Fiction. 3. Post-traumatic stress disorder—Fiction.
4. Family life—Fiction. 5. High schools—Fiction. 6. Schools—Fiction.] I. Title.
PZ7.S4195Mir 2012
[Fic]—dc22
2011008655
ISBN 978-1-4424-1707-6 (pbk)
ISBN 978-1-4424-1708-3 (eBook)

Acknowledgments

As always, many thanks to my editor, Jennifer Klonsky, for her amazingness, and a huge thank-you to everyone else at Simon Pulse and Simon & Schuster for being the best at what they do and for always making me feel like my book matters.

Hugs to the best copy editor around, Stephanie Evans, and to Robin, Beth, Diana, Ann, Jess, Amy, and everyone else who read through all the drafts and told me that I could do this.

Jay Asher, thank you for taking the time to read this book, and for then giving me such an amazing gift.

A shout-out to the best mailing list members any author could dream of: Brittany Conlon, Lexi Welch, Jenny Davies, Adrianne Russell, Brittney Tabel, Katrina Schofield, Christi Aldellizzi, Kaitlin Lyngaas, Vong Bidania, Nancy Woodford, Vanessa Ealum, Julie Kao, Samantha Townsend, Lucile Ogie-Kristianson, Mahlail Shahid, Andrea Burdette, and Hannah Joy Herring.

Finally, a very special thank-you to Yani Hernandez, who I think deserves a week of her own.

One

When I woke up the sky was burning.

It was orange-red with flames, breathing hot all over me, and thick black smoke bloomed like clouds. I rose to my knees and the sky grew hotter and closer as water poured over me. I knew I should turn around, that there was something behind me. I didn't know how I knew that. I just did.

I didn't turn around, and in front of me, through the bright flame of the sky, I saw a hint of green. I started walking toward it. Smoke was winding itself inside me, slipping down my throat every time I breathed.

My eyes hurt. My lungs hurt. I hurt. My feet caught on something and I fell.

My eyes were open, wide open, but I couldn't see anything.

After a while, it just seemed easier to close them. So I did.

Two

When I opened my eyes I saw light. Bright white light, so strong it made my eyes burn. I didn't know where I was, but then I smelled a weird yet familiar scent, disinfectant and sweat and used Band-Aids mixed together, and knew I'd fallen asleep in the hospital.

Great. What had David done now?

I tried to sit up. I couldn't. It hurt too much. I hurt too much.

There was an IV in each of my arms. I could see them stuck into my skin, taped into place well below the sleeves of my hospital gown.

I was the one in the hospital.

Why was I in the hospital? Had I gotten hurt during the last scrimmage at soccer camp? I'd been careful through every game there even though I'd known it meant I wouldn't get the best player award. I hadn't wanted to start the season with an injury.

I heard someone crying and tried to sit up again. It hurt even more this time. My head felt like it was filled with rocks. The crying got louder and then Mom was leaning over me, a huge, shaking smile lighting up her face. It looked strange, wrong against the tears.

"Mom?" I said, or tried to. Apparently there were rocks in my mouth too.

"Oh, Megan," Mom said, and her voice was weird, shaking just like her smile.

"Oh, Megan," she said again and behind her I saw a bright burning, knew that just past it—my mind went blank, frozen with something I didn't have a name for, and I stared at her, hoping she'd let me know why I was here. Let me know what had happened.

She put her hands on my shoulders, gently, touching me like I was made of glass. I could feel her fingers shaking. I could see that she was shaking. "George," she said, sobbing now, and then my father was there, his face creased with sleep.

"Meggie?" he said, and then he was hugging me so tight I could hardly breathe, squeezing me while he muttered, "It's a miracle. You're a miracle," over and over again.

I didn't know what was going on. Mom and Dad were

both crying, which scared me because Dad never cried. The day he and Mom first brought David home from the hospital his eyes were red and he kept clearing his throat, but he didn't cry. I did, and I was only seven and didn't even know what was wrong with David. Dad did, and he still didn't cry.

A doctor came in while Mom and Dad were still hugging me. I didn't recognize him and I should have because I knew every doctor in the Reardon Emergency Clinic. David practically lived there, first because he was sick all the time and then because he was always unable to ignore a tree that shouldn't be climbed or a patch of ice Dad hadn't scraped off the driveway.

The doctor didn't act like a doctor. He acted . . . strange. Too nice, and he kept saying my name like it was more than a name, like it meant something. "How's this light, Megan?" "Is it too bright, Megan?" "I'm going to take your blood pressure now, Megan, okay?"

I couldn't even focus on what he was doing, I hurt so much. I just kept hearing him say my name, over and over until it didn't even sound like a word.

"Remarkable," he said when he was done, smiling at me, and then turned to my parents. "She's in great shape. Some contusions, some bruising, and of course she's going to be sore for a while, but other than that—well, I've never seen anything like it."

Was he crazy? "I don't feel like I'm in great shape." My voice still sounded almost as bad as I felt.

Mom laughed, a strange high-pitched giggle that sounded like it was hiding a scream. "Sweetheart, you're in amazing shape. Just a few cuts and bruises—nothing worse than you've gotten during a soccer game."

She looked at the doctor. "I told you she'd be fine." Her voice sounded sure but brittle, and in her eyes I saw something that looked almost like fear.

The doctor nodded, looking at me and then at my parents again. "Well, Mr. and Mrs. Hathaway, while it does appear that her injuries from the crash are minimal, I'd like to consult with some specialists before making any decisions."

Crash? I was in a car accident? Oh God, Jess. She must have come to pick me up at the airport. I didn't remember it at all. Why didn't I? Was Jess—? I looked at my parents' tear-streaked faces and felt my heart clench.

"Is Jess okay?"

Mom blinked, the expression in her eyes shifting to something even more frightened for a second before it was smoothed away. "She's fine, sweetheart. Why wouldn't she be?"

"Can I see her? What about her car? Is it totaled?" Jess loved her car.

"Megan," my father said, taking my hand as the doctor

peered down at me, shining a light in my eyes. "Sweetheart, you were in an accident. But not with Jessica. Your plane crashed. You remember that, right?"

"What?"

The doctor clicked off the light. "In the Round Hills," he said. "In the forest. I hear you're real familiar with it, living out in Reardon. I guess that helped get you through it."

"Through what? I don't remember being on a plane that—I don't think I was in a . . ."

I rip open the tiny bag of pretzels with my teeth and stare out the rain-wet window at the clouds, which are gathering thick and dark. I saved the pretzels till now because the last part of the flight is so boring. Once you cross into Clark County it's all trees. The only reason Reardon even has an airport is because of the Park Service. Stupid forest. I remember how, on the flight out, when we took off the trees seemed so close to the plane, kind of like they are—

I shook my head. And then I started to cry.

Three

I'd been in the hospital for almost two days, and I wasn't in Reardon at all. I was all the way upstate in Staunton, in the LaMotte Memorial Medical Center, which I'd heard of because Rose from church went there after she got diagnosed with breast cancer. She died there too, last winter, and getting her body flown back to Reardon took days because of snowstorms. I didn't know why I kept thinking about that, but I did.

I couldn't remember the crash.

I said I did, though.

I said I did because I got tired of the doctor asking me if I did, of Mom and Dad looking worried, fear in their eyes as they clutched at me and smiled, wet-eyed. I thought about David and how they already worried so much about him.

How they kept saying I was fine like they needed it to be true.

I thought saying I remembered would make things better.

It didn't. The doctor came in less but Mom and Dad kept looking at me, kept smiling so much and so hard I was afraid they'd strain something. Every time I moved, Mom would let out a little sigh and then squeeze my hand. Dad kept hugging me.

It started to freak me out because they were acting like I'd become someone else, like I wasn't just Megan, their daughter, anymore. And they wouldn't leave me. Not to call David ("He's fine! We talked to him while the doctor was with you!"), not to get something to eat ("We're fine! We grabbed a sandwich earlier! The hospital cafeteria is very nice!"), not even to get some fresh air ("We just want to be here with you! Our (pause for smile and/or tears) miracle!"). I finally told them I wanted to go to the bathroom just to get some time away from them.

They had to help me walk there, and I was surprised at how far away it seemed, but kept going as they both peered anxiously at me while smiling and telling me how well I was doing. How fantastic I was.

The bathroom itself was small and a strange industrial yellow but the door locked, and I was finally alone.

Mom and Dad had both been in there. Mom had her makeup bag sitting on the back of the sink, and Dad had propped a razor and a can of shaving cream on top of it too. He'd also left a folded newspaper on top of the toilet tank. I picked it up, and my face stared back at me.

Girl Survives Plane Crash, Walks To Safety

By Gina Worshon

In what can only be termed a miracle, a survivor of Flight 619 somehow walked out of the Round Hills National Forest and then flagged down a passing motorist.

Megan Hathaway (pictured right), a rising senior at Reardon High and star soccer player who was returning from training camp when the plane crashed, waved down Joyce Johnson on her way to work.

"I don't normally stop for hitchhikers," Mrs. Johnson said, "but this girl was standing in the middle of the road. She didn't even have shoes on. I thought maybe she'd been attacked."

Miss Hathaway was pronounced dead by the Sheriff's Office over thirty-six hours earlier, and her parents, arriving in Staunton to learn of their daughter's final moments, instead found out she was alive. Miss

Hathaway is currently at LaMotte Memorial Medical Center, where she is being held for observation. She is expected to make a full recovery.

Flight 619 crashed in Round Hills National Forest shortly after it began its descent toward the Reardon airport. Rescue crews were sent out but ran into problems battling a thunderstorm. It took them over twelve hours to reach the plane and when they did, according to the party leader, Staunton's own Sheriff Andrew Green, they found no survivors.

"We did all we could," Green said when asked how Miss Hathaway hadn't been found. "No one should have been able to walk away from that crash. Miss Hathaway truly is a miracle."

Right below that was another, smaller article. *Memorial Service Unites Families in Grief.* I started to look at it, but my eyes froze as soon as I read:

Family, friends, and members of the community all turned out to remember Flight 619 victims: Park Service employees Walter Pelt, 24, and Sandra Lee, 27, as well as Clark resident Carl Brown, 52, and pilot Henry Roberts, 65.

Victims.

The dead.

I dropped the paper on the floor. I opened the door. Mom and Dad were right there, waiting for me. After they helped me back into bed I asked them what happened to the clothes I'd been wearing.

Mom looked at Dad. Dad looked at Mom. At first I thought they didn't want me to see them but as they looked at each other, then at me, I realized they'd been waiting for this. That they wanted it.

Dad went over to the far side of the room and picked up a plastic bag. He carried it just like he did the Bible when he was the lay reader at church and it made my skin crawl. He put the bag on my lap.

It was open, and inside were my shorts and my shirt. They were filthy. I didn't want to touch them.

I looked at Mom and Dad. They were watching me, waiting. I pulled the shirt out of the bag. It smelled like forest, like dirt and the sharp bite of the pines that grow around here, and there was a dark brown-red stain on it, dried blood. I wondered how deeply I'd been cut, and where. I looked down at myself but I was just a blur, hospital gown, toes tucked in tight under blankets. I tried to remember my face, my neck, myself in the bathroom mirror, but it wouldn't come.

"It's not your blood," Mom said, her voice high, nervous. "We saw you, when the ambulance came in, and at first we thought . . ." She shook her head. "But you were all right. You were fine. Just fine."

"We made it," I tell him, "we're all right," but he doesn't blink, doesn't move, and when I go back to him there is nothing to feel in his throat and his skin is wet and cooling. The rain smells like metal, like blood, and keeps pouring into his open eyes, making tears. I lean over his face, covering him from the rain, watching his eyes as I wipe his mouth with my shirt. He doesn't blink. His chest doesn't rise and fall. He doesn't see that we have lived.

"Come on," I say, pleading, but he doesn't answer.

Mom's hand cupped my chin. "Meggie, you're fine," she said, and her eyes welled with tears. "You're a miracle."

"I'm really tired," I said, and pushed the clothes away. "Do you think it would be okay if I slept for a while?"

I didn't think I'd sleep but I did. The last thing I remembered was opening my eyes to see if Mom and Dad were still there. If they were still watching me.

They were.

Four

In the morning I was released from the hospital. Someone came in to talk to me first. A counselor. Her name was Donna, and she had the whitest, brightest smile I'd ever seen.

She sat down next to me and said, "I've been looking forward to speaking to you," in a voice so bright and interested that I flinched, yet another person eager for me. She wanted to know what I was thinking about and when Mom said, "She's thinking she's glad to be going home," Donna asked her and Dad to leave, said they should come back in an hour.

When they were gone she asked me again how I was feeling ("Fine"), how I was sleeping ("Fine"), and if I had anything I wanted to "share." I thought about telling the truth, that the visit wasn't necessary since I couldn't remember anything, but she was leaning forward, staring at me like whatever I was going to say would change her life.

It freaked me out. Her questions, her staring, and I wished—

I wished Mom and Dad would stop looking at me like Donna was.

"Are you sure there's nothing you want to share?" she asked again.

"I'm tired of Jell-O," I said.

She smiled and said, "You seem very calm, Megan." It didn't exactly sound like a compliment and I don't think it was one because then she asked me about the memorial service and said, "Would you like to have gone?"

I nodded. She asked if I wanted to talk about the crash and when I shook my head she said, "Sharing the experience will help you heal."

And then she just sat there. She was still leaning forward, still staring at me, and it was like she wanted to eat everything I said. Like she was hungry for what was inside my head and I didn't like that. I didn't like her.

I didn't like any of this.

Mom came in then, looking tense. "I'm sorry to interrupt," she said, "but we're anxious to take Megan home and you seem to be—she looks upset."

"Megan and I have only spoken for a few minutes," Donna

said. "I was just going to ask her about her walk through Round Hills."

"Her walk?" Mom said, voice rising, carrying, and Dad came in then. He said, "Meggie has been through enough and we don't need you bothering her. We'll be leaving now. Thank you for your time."

Donna looked at my parents and then at me. "I think you might benefit from talking to someone," she told me. "Where do you live?"

"Reardon."

Donna blinked. "Oh," she said. "I can give you the name of someone in Derrytown."

Derrytown is eighty-five miles away and I think we all knew that wasn't going to happen. She gave me her card as she left anyway and said, "Please know you can call me."

I held it like it hurt my hand and Dad threw it away, then hugged me hard. "We're gonna take you home, baby girl," he said. "Everyone's waiting to see you."

We left in a car that wasn't ours, Mom and Dad and me hidden behind the tinted windows of a minivan. The driver, who worked for the hospital, told us we were heading to a rest stop out on the highway where we'd pick up Dad's truck so no reporters would follow us.

As we drove away, I saw reporters standing outside the

hospital, leaning against vans painted with television station logos. There were so many of them.

Some of them were giving reports, lights shining on them as they smiled.

"I understand you turned down all media requests," the driver said. I shivered, and Mom nodded, smiling briefly. "We did. We just want to get Meggie home and get back to our normal lives."

That sounded good, but all the way home she and Dad kept looking at me, like they were afraid that if they didn't, I'd be gone.

I stared out the windshield, telling myself things would be okay when we got home. I saw the forest, the sharp rise of the hills. I'd walked across them. I'd been in a plane that had crashed into them. I'd lived, and I didn't remember any of the people who'd died.

I didn't remember anything.

We got to Reardon in the afternoon, and I could see people at our house as soon as we turned onto our street. They were standing on the lawn, in the driveway, on the front porch, and it seemed like they all waved at once, a sea of hands and reaching arms, and as soon as I got out of the car, people started hugging me. I saw Mom and Dad, both of them crying again, as I was passed from one hug to another. I knew all the faces I saw, of course, but it was strange to see so many of them so fast.

I finally got to see David, who didn't hug me but instead just stared at me, his eyes wide. He'd managed to cut his forehead, and the bandage someone had put on it was already starting to come off.

"What happened to your hair?"

"Nothing," Mom said, putting an arm around me and pulling me close. "The doctors just had to cut it a little."

I reached up and touched it. It was a lot shorter than I remembered. I have my dad's hair, brown and thick, and I'd grown it out so it hit the small of my back. At soccer camp I'd been able to wind it up and tuck it into a bun without any clips, feel the heavy weight resting low on my neck. Now it barely reached my shoulders and the ends were brittle, snapping off when I touched them.

It was burnt. My hair had been . . . it had been on fire. I'd seen myself in mirrors at the hospital, I knew I had. How had I not seen this? How had I not seen myself?

"What else is wrong with me?" I asked, scrabbling my fingers over my neck, feeling for blisters, raw patches. All I felt was skin.

"Nothing, Meggie, nothing," Mom said, stilling my hand with hers. "You're fine, perfectly fine. David, run along inside, please."

"But, Mom, I—" David said, his voice fading as more people crowded around me. I was hugged again, this time by

Jess and Lissa, both of them talking over each other so fast I couldn't understand a word they said. They smelled like suntan lotion and chlorine from Lissa's pool. They smelled like summer. Like normal. I hugged them back, hard.

"Oh my God, Meggie," Jess said, waving her boyfriend, Brian, over. "When we heard what happened and saw pictures of the plane—"

"But then we saw pictures of you," Lissa said, and then they were both crying and laughing at the same time, smiling so broad Jess's dimples were stretched tight and Lissa's braces glinted bright in the sun. I felt strange, like the ground under me wasn't quite real and was glad to be pulled away, hugged by Brian and then Mom's boss and then some of the guys on Dad's softball team.

I heard someone ask Mom if she'd heard from her parents and watched her shake her head, frowning for a moment before she looked over at me. The frown turned into a smile but the expression in her eyes wasn't happy. She looked almost frightened.

"All right, everyone," Dad said, coming up behind Mom and wrapping his arms around her and me. "What do you say we all go inside? The church set up a buffet, and Meggie hasn't had anything to eat but hospital food for days." He grinned at me. "I bet real food sounds good right about now, doesn't it?"

I nodded, and everyone started heading inside.

The whole town seemed to be in our house and by the time I'd made it halfway across the kitchen I was light-headed.

I made it to the kitchen table, where Reverend Williams led everyone in a prayer and then people took turns talking about how amazing I was. How brave I was. What a miracle I was.

I kept touching my hair, finding burnt pieces and snapping them off. David ran through the kitchen, the bandage on his forehead gone, showing a deep gash that started in his hair and ran all the way down to right above his left eyebrow. I waited for Mom to get up and run after him with the hydrogen peroxide and first aid kit, but she stayed where she was, next to me with one hand stroking down the length of my back.

"I'm happy to be home," I said over and over again, until it sounded like less than words, like it was nothing. "I'm just so happy."

The thing was, I didn't feel happy.

I didn't feel anything.

Dad excused himself, glancing at Mom as he got up from the table, and I watched as he went over to our next-door neighbor, Mr. Reynolds, who was obviously drunk, stood swaying and holding a picture in his hands. Dad said something to him, and Mr. Reynolds pointed at the picture. Dad looked behind him, frowning, and then I saw the back of Joe's neck as he came over to his father and walked him to the door. Lots of heads turned as he left, all female, and I saw a couple of girls move toward the living room window so they could look at Joe walking his father home.

The person who was hugging me took my face in their hands, turning me toward them. I heard the words "precious" and "wonderful" and "God's will." My skin felt smeared and rubbery, and I said I had to use the bathroom. People actually cleared a path for me as I walked to it. I saw Lissa and waited for her to laugh or roll her eyes but she just stepped back along with everyone else.

When I got into the bathroom I shut the door and then stood there staring at myself in the mirror. I looked fine. Like I had a bad haircut, but fine. How could someone like me survive a plane crash? I didn't look like someone who could do that.

I wasn't someone who could do that.

Maybe I hadn't. Maybe I was dead. Maybe I was lying on the ground somewhere, rain falling over me, into my open eyes. I looked at myself in the mirror and didn't see anything. Didn't see me. I leaned forward and rested my head against the sink. It was cold.

I took a deep breath and then another, the way I did before a game, when I needed to focus. It didn't work. I felt like I was outside myself, like I wasn't in my body. I felt like I could see myself standing slumped over the sink, and that any second my body would fall over and stop moving, stop breathing. Stop everything.

I felt like I was lost from myself, like I wasn't really here. What if the reason why I couldn't remember anything was because none of this was real? What if I wasn't real?

I knew I was breathing but yet I was sure, somehow, that I wasn't. The sink suddenly smelled like smoke, like burning, and I stood up so fast I had to lean against the wall, dizzy.

I knew I was alive then. Dead people didn't get dizzy. Dead people didn't feel like they weren't breathing when they were.

I did.

And I didn't know why.

Why had I lived?

And why—why wasn't I happy about it?

I don't know how I got through the next couple of hours. I waded through all the people crowded into our downstairs, pasting a smile on my face as they talked at me, hugged me more. I ate pasta salad and potato salad and gelatin salad and cake and a chicken casserole that Margaret, who lived right across from the church, had brought over.

"Try it," she said as she handed me a plate, her old-lady arms flapping around in her T-shirt. "Someone brought it over after the funeral last year and I asked if I could have the recipe."

"After Rose's funeral?" I hadn't meant to say it out loud but it was the first time someone had said something to me that wasn't about what had happened. That wasn't about me. Margaret and Rose were best friends and had lived together until Rose passed away.

Margaret nodded and squinted at me from behind her glasses.

"I know a doctor you might want to go see," she said. "Nice enough, for a doctor, and his practice isn't too far away either. Dr. Lincoln. He knows a lot about trauma and maybe you'd like to talk to him."

"I can't," I said, thinking of Donna and her staring, of how I had no idea how I'd lived or why, and Margaret squinted at me again.

"Can't?"

"Can't what?" Dad said, coming over and helping himself to some of Margaret's casserole. "This looks great, as always."

"Thank you, George. I was just telling Meggie about a doctor I know who deals with a lot of trauma cases. I could give you his number or—"

"I think Meggie's seen more than enough doctors," Dad said. "Hospital was full of 'em! And besides, she's safe now and at home where she belongs. We'll look out for her, and that's the most important thing. Besides, we have Dr. Weaver, remember?"

Margaret nodded, frowning, and then turned away as Reverend Williams called her name, beckoning her to his side. She and Rose had always volunteered at church, and Margaret still did, basically doing everything except delivering sermons.

I'd liked Rose. She'd looked like a grandmother, short and fat with white hair and a big smile. She baked cookies and always wore sweatshirts that said things like OVER FIFTY BUT NOT OVER THE HILL. She refused to drive anywhere, yet somehow always managed to show up whenever you needed a helping hand. When David first came home she brought a month's worth of meals, all neatly packaged, and said he was adorable. She sounded like she meant it, and I think she did even though he looked like a raisin.

That night, when it was quiet, I couldn't sleep. I lay there, sure I wouldn't, and then woke up with a start, something hot stinging my eyes and throat.

I lay there for a long time, trying to go back to sleep, but I could hear the trees rustling outside and I didn't like the way they sounded. Plus whenever I closed my eyes, I saw a bright red sky.

After a while it felt better to just make myself stay awake, to stare up at my dark ceiling. To remind myself I was at home, in my room.

To remind myself I was alive.

Five

In the morning, Mom took me to see Dr. Weaver.

On our way there she said, "I know you're completely fine. It's just that I'd feel better having Dr. Weaver give you a checkup, and besides, you'd be going to see him around now before you went back to school anyway, right?"

I shrugged. Dr. Weaver had been our family doctor forever. Mom loved him because he'd done so much for David, but I didn't like him much. He was maybe a few years older than Dad, but he was cranky like he was a hundred. He always talked to Mom about me like I wasn't there and if I said anything, he would glance at me, one eyebrow raised, and then turn back to Mom.

But this time he came into the room early, before the nurse even arrived, and waved her away when she did, taking my blood pressure and temperature himself. He said my cuts were healing and that my bruises were already starting to fade.

Everything was normal. He said that twice.

"I was sorry to miss your homecoming, Meggie," he said. "I was over in Clark, visiting family."

"Oh," I said, because I didn't know what else to say, and saw the nurse out in the hallway, head tilted toward my voice. I saw Dr. Weaver looking me, his eyes curious and eager. *Tell me about the crash*, they both seemed to be saying. *Tell me your story, let me hear what a miracle you are. Let me be a part of it.*

"I have to use the bathroom," I said, and got up.

I didn't go to the bathroom. I went out to the waiting room, still in my jeans and the paper smock I'd had to put on over my bra, and stared at the door. There were trees outside, green and tall. It seemed like they were watching me. Waiting for me.

I sat down, feeling sweat pool in my armpits, across my back. The receptionist stared at me.

"Are you all right?" she asked, sounding bored, and then I saw her expression change, her eyes widen.

"Megan Hathaway," she breathed, like my name was special, and came out from behind her desk. I watched her talk but didn't listen, just nodded and let her take me down the hall and back to Dr. Weaver. He and Mom were talking about the crash and as Dr. Weaver motioned for me to sit back down the receptionist joined in, the nurse poking her head in too.

"I couldn't believe it when I saw the pictures. The plane, it was just—"

"Completely destroyed. And then I heard that Megan was on it and I—"

"Said to my wife, 'Look, that's one of my patients. Wonderful girl, very—'"

"Miraculous. When George and I got the call, we just . . . there aren't words to describe it. They said she was gone. And then we drove to Staunton and she—" Mom took a breath and the room was so quiet, too quiet, and when I blinked I saw something different, a long narrow corridor with airline blue seats and—

"Can we leave?" I said, the words coming out in a rush, and I grabbed the edge of my paper smock with both hands, my fingers breaking through it.

On the drive home, Mom kept asking me how I felt. I think she knew something was going on with me. But I could tell from the way her hand shook when she smoothed my hair, and from how desperately hopeful her eyes were, that she needed me to be okay. I knew she'd been told I'd died, but I hadn't really thought about it until then. I hadn't thought about what it must have done to her.

"I'm fine," I said, as we waited for a tractor to cross the road, and saw her relax, saw her take a deep breath like she hadn't been able to breathe properly before.

And I would be fine. I just had to stop thinking about the crash. I had to stop worrying about why I couldn't remember it. I had to stop worrying about why I'd lived. I had to stop feeling weird about being called a miracle. It was just another word, and people used it to talk about things like shampoo. I was still me, and that was what mattered.

But when I crawled into bed that night and closed my eyes, I saw a burning sky and didn't sleep again.

I lay there, staring out my window up at the sky, and I couldn't escape the thought that I didn't feel much like myself anymore. I didn't feel much like anything.

Then school started a few days later, and things got worse.

Jess and Lissa were waiting for me when I left the house, full of homemade waffles and tired of watching David run around trying to get Mom or Dad to notice that he'd given himself a haircut with the scissors Dad used to trim his beard.

"Hey!" they both said, and hugged me. Then Jess showed me an orange spot on her neck, said, "Look what Brian did last night. Can you tell I have a hickey? Is this foundation too orange for me?"

Jess never asked me about makeup. Or hickeys. We

both knew I knew practically nothing about either of those things.

I nodded.

"See?" Lissa said. "I told you. Meggie, what do you think of my outfit?"

Lissa never asked me what I thought about her clothes. Lissa's parents, who'd "retired" to Reardon after they'd made a lot of money starting some computer company, went to New York twice a year on vacation, and Lissa always came back with clothes no one else would have until the Target in Derrytown started selling knockoffs months later.

"Just don't mention her butt," Jess said, laughing. "She's obsessing about it again. Oh, I like your flip-flops!"

"They are nice," Lissa said. "Where did you get them?"

I stared at Lissa. Since when had I had any fashion sense at all? "Mom got them for me."

She had. She'd also bought me a new pair of soccer cleats. I didn't know why, but I didn't want to look at them, and after she gave them to me, I threw them in the trash. She took them out, smiling as she reminded me to check shopping bags before I threw them away, and put them in my closet. Now they were on the roof.

I'd realized a lot of stuff about my room when I was supposed to be sleeping, like the fact that if I opened my window and climbed out, I could swing down onto the porch. I hadn't tried it, but I'd thought about it.

I could also fling stuff up over my head and hear it land on the roof. I had tried that. So far the cleats were there, and an afghan made by volunteers at the Staunton hospital. They'd made it the color of the forest, different shades of green, to remind me of my "amazing courage." I hated it.

"So," Jess said, and pointed at her neck again. "Is this color really okay?"

It was like that all day. Lissa and Jess wanted to know what I thought about everything. Everyone wanted to know what I thought. Everyone wanted to say hi to me, to hug me, to tell me how great it was to see me. It was nice, I told myself, and tried to be happy.

It didn't work.

After school Lissa said, "Call me when you get home from practice," and Jess said, "Yeah, call me too, okay?"

As I walked down to the field, I could feel the whole team looking at me. Then they started clapping, and Coach Henson smiled at me. He never smiled. He frowned and yelled stuff like, "Is that the best you can do?"

"This," he said, pointing at me as I started to sit down, "is what you all need to strive to be like. Meggie doesn't quit. She doesn't ever give up."

Everyone clapped again. I started to feel weird again, like I wasn't in my body even though I knew I was.

"Why don't you get us started on our warm-up laps?" Coach said, and everyone looked at me, waiting. Watching.

"I—I can't," I said. "I just remembered I have to do something at home."

It took everything I had to walk off the field normally, to keep whatever was inside me pushed down enough to act like I was fine when I just wanted to run and run until I couldn't think, until I was far away. Until I was away from myself.

Coach called that night, and after I told him I needed a break from soccer and hung up, Mom and Dad agreed that they respected my choice. Mom had said stuff like that before, but what she'd meant then was she respected my choices as long as they were the ones she wanted. As for Dad, well, he loved that I played soccer. David, for all his fort-building and tree-climbing and bone-cracking, wasn't very athletic. He was slight and clumsy and got sick so easily that putting him on a team just meant there'd be more days of school he'd have to miss, more colds he'd suffer through.

"Meggie, whatever you want to do is fine with me," Mom said, and Dad nodded, added, "You have to do what's right for you, sweetheart." Then they both hugged me.

That's when I knew things weren't ever going to get back to

normal. My parents hugged me plenty, but they'd always given parent hugs, those squeezes that make you feel safe but also judge a little, a reminder that you're still loved but the fact you forgot to take out the trash has been noticed.

Now they hugged me like I was made of glass. Not like I might break, but like I was something priceless. They didn't hug me like they used to and that's when I knew I wasn't Meggie anymore. I wasn't even Megan.

I was Miracle.

I didn't know what to do. I kept getting up in the morning, kept going to school, and kept doing homework. Kept doing all the things I'd always done. But in the mornings now, I didn't have to eat cereal bars while Mom fussed over David, feeling his forehead or asking him how he felt. Instead I ate waffles and bacon and orange juice and when David wiped his runny nose on his sleeve Mom said, "Sweetie, use a napkin, please," and asked me if I wanted anything else.

At school, the popular people, the ones whose parents were supervisors at Reardon Logging, didn't ask me to sit with them at lunch, but they said hi to me in the halls and asked me what I was doing on the weekends. Sometimes they even invited me to their parties and once I said, "I can't," a couple of times, they started asking me even more. In class, my teachers said, "Good job," even when I answered a question wrong, and I passed every test and quiz I took, even when I left every answer blank.

Jess and Lissa also finally asked about the crash. I'd been waiting for it, and as soon as they did I realized I'd been hoping they would ask something different. That they would somehow see that I was different and want to know why. But they just wanted to know the same things everyone else did, wanted to know what I'd thought, how I'd survived. They wanted to hear how amazing I was. Find out how I'd become a miracle.

I kept the story short. I had to. I still didn't remember the crash or what had happened afterward. But what little I said made them smile, made them look at me like I was their best friend.

The thing was, Jess and Lissa had always been better friends with each other than with me. But now I was the one they turned to first, and every day after school I decided what we would do. They should have hated me for wanting to sit in Lissa's or Jess's house and watch television and not go anywhere, but they didn't. Everything I wanted to do was a great idea. Everything I said was interesting.

I knew I should care about that. That I should hate how weird things were or maybe like it, enjoy being the center of our friendship. But I didn't hate it. I didn't like it. I didn't care.

I didn't care about anything.

In church the Sunday after I'd told Jess and Lissa what they wanted to hear, Reverend Williams talked about miracles.

Everyone was quiet when he finished speaking, and he smiled at me. Mom squeezed one of my hands and Dad squeezed the other. I sat there and wondered again why I'd lived. Why I didn't even feel like I was here.

The organ started the hymn we were supposed to sing and the opening notes were loud, booming, and my heart lurched, pounded hard and fast. I gasped and twitched like I was having some sort of fit and the organ faltered, Margaret hitting a wrong note.

When I looked at her she was watching me, unsmiling.

After church there was a covered dish supper. I ate baked ham and mashed potatoes and cake and sat with Jess and Brian. Behind them I could see my parents, chatting with everyone around them as they watched me. I heard David, his loud "ha!" of a laugh rising up over everyone else's voices, and Mom and Dad still looked at me instead of checking on him. Before we left, I promised Jess I'd call her when I got home.

When we did, I didn't call her. Instead I fell asleep on the sofa, exhausted from all the nights I'd lain awake reminding myself that I was home. That I was safe. That I was alive.

I dreamed I was running through a forest, pushing past trees licked with flame into deeper, darker woods, running and running as I heard the flames grow closer, urging me to turn back, to wait for them. But I wouldn't. I couldn't. They caught me though, held me tight, and I wrenched my eyes open with a start, muffling a cry as I slipped off the sofa and onto the floor.

When I landed, the side of my face hit one of David's toys. He saw it—he was sitting there watching TV—and froze. Both of us did, but then my right eye started to swell shut. I went and stood in the bathroom with my hands clutching my arms, staring at it, at the skin around it turning that dark inky purple-blue the sky sometimes gets at night, and then I poked it over and over until my eyes watered so much I could hardly see a thing.

David knocked on the bathroom door and said, "Are you okay?" I ignored him even when he said it again and rubbed my eyes one more time, making the right one burn, and then opened the door.

I didn't say anything to David, and he didn't say anything either. He just stared at me.

"You're acting like a freak," he finally said. "You're all quiet and weird."

Dad heard that and yelled at him—I kept my head down so I wouldn't have to hear anything about my eye—and when Mom came in, she got upset too and decided she and David and Dad needed to have a talk.

"About Meggie?" David said.

"No, about you," Mom said and Dad nodded, adding, "That's right, son. Your behavior—wait a minute. Did you cut your hair?"

David smiled and I realized it was the first time he had all day. It was also the first time Mom and Dad had noticed the haircut he'd given himself. The one he'd done days ago.

I went upstairs and looked out the window. Even though one eye was swollen shut, I could still see the trees. There were too many of them, and I didn't like how close they were. I lay down on my bed and watched them.

Six

School was a joke with my eye. I didn't have to do much before and now I didn't have to do anything. Coach Henson pulled me out of chemistry to ask how I was doing and ended up taking me to the principal's office, where the secretary showed me a scrapbook the school was putting together about me. They were going to put it in the display case by the auditorium, in with all the trophies.

I said I needed to get back to class—the thought of me, singled out like that, made me feel sick—and Coach Henson said, "Good, good, keep up those grades and come sit in on a practice whenever you want, all right?"

"Okay," I said but I wasn't going to practice. Not again. I just . . . I couldn't.

When I got home after school, I went straight to bed,

exhausted from not sleeping, and woke up when David stood in my doorway and yelled, "Dinner!"

"Okay," I said, sitting up and rubbing my eyes before I remembered.

"We're having BLTs again because they're your favorite," he said as I winced, my right eye hurting, and stomped downstairs.

Dinner was quiet. Or was until David said, "Mom, why did you spend forever staring at Meggie when you got home?"

"What?" I said.

"You weren't even doing anything," David said to me, picking the tomatoes and lettuce out of his sandwich. "But I had to be quiet so you could sleep."

"Whatever, David. You know Mom wouldn't tell you to . . ." I trailed off, shocked by the anger in his eyes. I looked at Mom and knew he was right. She'd watched me sleep and that . . . that was beyond weird. She'd watched me sleep and hadn't asked about my eye, as if talking about it would make me somehow not perfect, not a miracle, and now she was looking at me with that happy and yet terrified look in her eyes, the one that had been there since I woke up in the hospital.

I wanted it—Mom's look, how I felt, everything—to stop so badly but it hadn't. And it wouldn't.

I got up from the table and went out onto the deck. Mom

and Dad came out to join me right away and my insides cramped. David came too, carrying my soccer ball. Mom and Dad both said, "Put that back!" at the same time.

"It's okay," I said. "He can use it."

David stared at me, then frowned furiously and kicked the ball as hard as he could. He didn't swing his leg right though, and the ball popped over our fence and landed in Joe's yard. It came back over right away, on the wings of a muttered curse, and I saw the top of Joe's head. A minute later, I heard music, so loud the boards of the deck shook a little.

"Goodness," Mom said, looking at Dad.

"I'll call over there. Ron's truck is in the driveway, so he's probably home," he said, and went into the house. Two minutes later, Joe came back outside.

"You could have just asked me to turn it down," he said to all of us, looking over the fence from David to me to Mom and Dad and then back to me. "What the hell happened to you?"

"She survived a plane crash," my mother said sharply.

"No, I mean your eye," Joe said, looking at me. "You didn't have it before, and why are you poking at it like that?"

I froze and realized my fingers were by my eye, pressing into the soft bruise around it.

"Let's go inside and get some ice for that," Mom said.

"David, come do your homework. Joe, please tell your father we said hello."

"Right," Joe said. "He'll be thrilled."

Joe and his parents moved next door when I was four and he was six. They'd lived all the way across town before that, but moved because they needed more room. Or at least that's what they said. They actually moved because Joe's grandmother kicked them out of her house in order to sell it and move to Alabama. Everyone knew that. There are plenty of people who don't speak to each other in Reardon, just like in any other town, but it's small enough so that everyone knows everyone else's business eventually.

We'd helped our other neighbors at the end of the street move in, and I was even allowed to carry the cake Mom had made to welcome them. We didn't do anything like that for Joe and his family. My parents didn't like them. No one in town did. Mr. Reynolds had lost a thumb and his job at Reardon Logging in an accident he caused that had also killed four people, and that's not the kind of thing people forgive. He didn't work for years after that, not until after his daughter, Beth, died, and even then he could only get a job with a company in Clark as a trucker.

Mrs. Reynolds moved away soon after Beth's funeral. She started living with a bartender outside of Derrytown and was supposedly saving up money for a divorce. She never came back to town, not to visit Beth's grave, not even when Joe finally came back home from military school.

Beth was born about a year after David was and she was adorable, a chubby, happy baby like the ones you see in ads, and she grew into an adorable kid. Everyone in town loved her in spite of the rest of her family. She was also really smart. I can remember seeing her sitting at the end of her driveway waiting for Joe to get off the school bus when she was about four. When David and I got off they were already walking toward their house but I heard them talking. Joe was reading problems from his math book to her.

"One-half plus three-quarters equals what?" he said. "See, what you do is—"

"Five-fourths," she said. "What did you have for lunch?"

When she finally started school, no one knew what to do with her. She probably should have been in high school, but who would send a five-year-old there? So she went to school with kids her own age but basically got to do her own thing. Right before she died, she was reading thick novels written by authors I'd never heard of and solving math problems that had just as many letters as numbers.

After she died, the whole town turned out for her funeral, and so many people wanted to share their memories that the service lasted for hours. Six months after that, Joe went off to a military school near where his grandma lived. Everyone said his mom sent him so she could move out and live with the bartender. Joe had come back the month before I left for soccer camp, tanned and dressed in a military-looking uniform that was in the trash on the curb the morning after he got back, and got a job working at Reardon Logging. There was a lot of talk about that. That, and how he was out all the time and all the girls he was seen with.

Joe always had girls following him around, and it wasn't because he was popular or funny or anything like that. He was just beautiful. Guys aren't usually beautiful, but there was no other word for Joe. He had the same things everyone else had—a nose, eyes, a mouth—and there was nothing out of the ordinary about any of them. But put all together, there was just something about him that made you want to look at him. It was like you couldn't help yourself.

I'd spoken to him exactly nine times.

1. A "Hi" the day he moved in. We'd both said that.

2. He said, "No," when I asked him if he wanted to come over and play the next week. My parents saw me ask him and told me not to do it again.

3. Which, of course, made me ask the next day. He said, "Play what?" I said, "I don't know."

4. He said, "So why'd you ask?" Again, my reply: "I don't know."

5. Naturally, of course, I decided I liked him after that and even told him so. "I like you," I said. He said, "So?" And that was that.

6. He said, "Hi," to me when I was seven and we were both waiting, shivering, at the end of the road for the school bus to pick us up because the town still hadn't been able to send the volunteer fire department/rescue squad/snow removal crew around to clear all the streets.

7. When I was nine, he threw a baseball over our fence and said, "Thanks," when I took it back to him.

8. When I was thirteen he said, "Hey," to me right before he told Jimmy Hechts, a senior who was trying to get me to come sit with him in the back of the bus, "Damn, Jimmy, I know you're desperate, but at least pick someone who actually has breasts."

9. And last year, when I said, "I'm sorry," at Beth's funeral, he said, "Thanks," like a robot, his voice and expression totally blank.

Before I'd left for soccer camp I couldn't stop trying to catch glimpses of him. I was afraid to talk to him, but I never got tired of looking at him. Even Mom noticed him when he'd come outside to mow the lawn his second day home. Jess and I had been watching him out the kitchen window. He wasn't wearing a shirt, and we'd both pretty much had our faces pressed up against the glass.

"Girls, honestly," Mom had said, and then "Oh," when she'd actually looked over and saw him, blushing as she twitched the curtains closed and asked Jess about Brian.

I'd thought about Joe a lot before I'd left for camp, the kind of thoughts that probably would have made Mom and Dad lock me in my room and forbid me from ever even looking next door again.

Now when I thought about Joe, I didn't feel anything.

I felt nothing all the time, and it had started to feel normal. It should have scared me, but it didn't. Instead I was tired, the kind of tired that drapes itself over you like a heavy coat, pressing you down and muffling the world.

School was too much effort, even when my eye got better. Jess and Lissa always wanted my attention. They would talk and I would watch them, their words collapsing into a loud buzzing noise. It was even worse with everyone else. Whenever someone talked to me, it was all I could do to just keep watching them. I wanted to look at the floor or, better yet, lie down and curl into it. I got by on nodding and tossing out a few words when I had to, but it took a lot and I just—eventually I stopped pretending I was even listening to anyone.

I could feel my body changing too, softening. I wasn't running around a practice field, wasn't getting up early every morning to jog. The soccer ball had joined my cleats up on the roof, wedged in among all the crap, and every morning I slept until Mom came and woke me up with a kiss. I was her bleary-eyed miracle, and I ate everything she made for me even if I wasn't hungry because at least then I knew there was something inside me.

It was easy enough to be Miracle Megan. Everything I did made Mom and Dad happy. Just sitting at the dinner table would make them grin at me through the whole meal and every day I got an offering: a magazine from Mom, a pint of my favorite ice cream brought home by Dad. A car.

The night Dad brought that home, a sleek and shiny red two-door that looked like a dream I was supposed to have, I stood clutching the keys and staring at it.

"Come on," Dad said, grinning at me. "Let's take it out, see what you think."

"I don't want it." I didn't. Just seeing it made me feel sick. I'd begged them for a car, back before everything changed, back before I was a miracle. They'd said they couldn't afford it.

"Oh," Dad said, glancing at Mom nervously.

"You're crazy," David told me. "Dad, I'll take the car! I promise I won't even drive it till I have my license."

"David, hush," Mom said and then turned to me. "Let's have dessert out on the deck."

We all went outside and she kept hugging me, pushing

my hair back from my face and staring into my eyes, and Dad kept squeezing my shoulders like he was making sure I was still there. They wouldn't stop, not even when David went back inside and yelled that he was up on the kitchen counter trying to get the chocolate chips.

It was a disaster waiting to happen but they didn't do anything but watch me like they had to, and so I went into the kitchen and hauled David off the counter.

"Idiot," I said, hissing the word because I was suddenly angry, a rush of red-hot fury filling me so fast it was like I was choking on it, and he just stood there. That made me even madder because didn't he know he needed to be careful? Why didn't he ever care if he got hurt? Didn't he know how easily it could happen?

He didn't know. He just stood there, stupid and lucky, and he had lived when he shouldn't have and never thought about it. Never wondered why. He just banged himself up, got hurt, and never thought about it, but one day he wouldn't be able to stop it, one day he'd open his eyes and see—

Red, burning, the sky on fire.

I hit him. I hadn't hit David since he was two and went around biting everything, including me, but I smacked him so hard my hand stung.

He stumbled, round-eyed with tears starting to shine in his

eyes, and then hit me back. His fists felt like nothing as I yanked him toward me, one hand tight in his hair, a red haze covering everything I saw and flooding through me. Driving me.

"Meggie! David! Meggie! DAVID!" Mom and Dad were both shouting, pulling us apart, and David and I were suddenly on opposite sides of the kitchen.

"She hit me!" David screamed, his face so red you couldn't see the mark of my fingers on it.

"Shut up," Mom said, and he did.

Mom never said "shut up." She thought it was rude, and had always told us so. "Your sister rushes into the kitchen to pull you off the counter, the counter you've been told not to climb up onto, and you hit her?"

"She HIT ME!" David screamed again, even louder. "And I always climb on the counter!"

He did. He wasn't supposed to, but he did. Just like he climbed trees and fell out of them, then promised he wouldn't before doing it again. That was how things were. He was the baby, the special one, the one Mom and Dad held tight and worried over even as they smiled and shook their heads because he was alive and was never supposed to be. He was their miracle.

"David Jacob," Mom said. "Go to your room. I'm too angry to look at you right now."

Was their miracle.

Seven

I ate a mountain of pancakes in the morning, their sweet fluffiness not filling me up or erasing David's angry eyes as he touched his face where I'd hit him, and went out to meet Jess and Lissa. They saw the car in the driveway and said I should have called and told them.

"I meant to," I said, but I hadn't and was pretty sure they knew it. I also knew they wouldn't say anything about it. Not now that I was a miracle.

"You know, Brian can change the oil and stuff," Jess said. "He's really good at it." Brian loved cars and wanted to work at the one garage in town. It was an impossible dream, as the garage had a mechanic who was twenty-five and who'd taken over just last year when his father, the previous mechanic, had died of a heart attack.

"Great. Thanks."

We rode in silence to school, but when we got there and out of Jess's car, Lissa cleared her throat.

Jess shot her a look and asked me, "So . . . what's going on with soccer? You haven't quit, have you?"

"I just need a break. I mean, I've been playing forever."

"Exactly," Lissa said. "You've been playing forever so it's kind of weird that you just stopped." She caught Jess's eye and added, "Not weird bad or anything. Just, you know, kind of strange."

"Strange?" I said.

"Different," Jess said hastily. "That's what Lissa meant. It's just different."

I nodded. "Right. Different."

I wasn't sad, standing there knowing they knew something was wrong with me but couldn't bring themselves to say it. I wasn't anything.

I looked at my two best friends, who knew everything about me, and it was like I was looking at strangers. People I could easily walk right by.

"Look, Meggie," Jess said and she didn't even look like Jess to me now. She was just a girl with brown curls dressed in jeans and a T-shirt, and I didn't—I didn't even miss the girl I used to see.

"I gotta go," I said and walked away. It was the only way I

could get through the day and even then it seemed to last forever. They both called that night, and I told Mom to tell them I was sleeping. I went to my room to "work on homework" and fell asleep when it was still light out.

I woke up shaking from a dream of a hand clutching mine under a burning sky.

Jess and Lissa came to pick me up again the next morning. I didn't want to deal with them, with how they'd gone from being my best friends to nothing.

"Hey, Dad, I haven't finished breakfast," I said, and he grinned at me over his paper. I was so sick of smiles. "Can you give me a ride to school?"

"Sure."

I went to the porch and yelled, "Dad's giving me a ride," then watched Jess and Lissa squint at me from inside the car.

"Meet by the soda machine before first period?" Jess said, sticking her head out the window.

"Sure."

"You'd better be there," Lissa yelled, grinning to show it wasn't a threat but a friend thing, a "we want to see you" thing. A "we have to talk" thing.

"Of course!" I yelled back, but I didn't meet them. I had Dad drop me off by the gym and went into the girls' locker room, empty during the day because Physical Education hadn't been offered since my parents were in high school due to budget problems.

I went to first period after the bell rang. The teacher didn't give me a tardy. Jess tried to get my attention, but I pretended I didn't see her and scribbled in my notebook, page after page of long, waving lines. After class, I stayed to talk to the teacher. Jess and Lissa hung around, waiting for me.

"Don't wait," I called out, and then turned away.

I made it through the rest of school, but that night Mom said, "Are you upset with Jess and Lissa?"

Lissa had just called, and I'd told Dad to tell her I was busy with homework. I'd already had Mom tell Jess the same thing.

I shook my head.

"Are you sure?"

I nodded.

"Is there anything you need?"

A way to avoid Jess and Lissa, I thought. A way to avoid everyone, to go where I was supposed to on my own . . .

"The car," I said. "Can I have the car?"

I could. Dad hadn't been able to talk the previous owner into taking it back, much less returning his money, and it had been sitting outside his office.

So I started driving. I didn't like it. In the car, the sky seemed much closer somehow, like it was pushing down into the road, and if I looked at it too long I got dizzy and was afraid I'd get sucked up into it, that it would slice open the car and take me.

But I drove. I drove myself to school, getting there in time to make first period just as the bell rang. I spent the rest of the day in the library, supposedly working on an independent study project on local history. I'd gotten Coach Henson to sign off on supervising it by saying I'd come back to soccer in a month.

Independent studies were normally given to the Walker kids, supersmart whiners who got to do them because their mother threatened to sue the school over the lack of AP classes. But I was an exception. I was very special. I was a miracle. My guidance counselor said all this and more when I sat in her office asking permission, Coach nodding along, and I smiled and said the thing was, I was going to need to do a lot of research and would have to be in the library during school, maybe even sometimes during a tiny bit of class, and I might sometimes do research outside of school.

"Well," Coach said, "I think it'll be all right just this once, don't you? I mean, this is Megan Hathaway who's asking."

It was all right. Of course it was.

Jess and Lissa tried to talk to me for a while, but I always realized I'd left something in the car or had to go see Coach or a teacher, and when they called, I was always busy or asleep.

And then one morning Lissa was waiting for me as I came into school, caught me as I was on my way to the girls' locker room. She was angry. I could tell just by looking at her.

"What's going on with you?" she said.

I shrugged. "Just busy."

"Look, Meggie, last night Brian told Jess he's giving her an engagement ring at graduation. We're going to my house after school to look at rings online and then she and Brian are going to the Walmart out in Derrytown this weekend to pick one out and put it on layaway."

"That's great."

"*That's great.* That's it? Jess is going to get engaged. I know Brian gave her a promise ring last year but this is different. She's going to be getting married. It's the biggest thing that will ever happen to her."

"I know."

She shook her head. "Yeah, you know. Now. But you won't be there after school today, will you? And if she tries to call and tell you what he said when he asked her to marry him, you'll be too busy or have a headache or David will say, 'She doesn't want to come to the phone. Bye.' You know, I'm sorry we didn't all survive plane crashes this summer, Meggie, because if we had then maybe we'd be good enough for you to actually talk to."

"Maybe," I said and heard the nothingness in my voice. The emptiness.

Lissa stared at me, and then she started to cry. Lissa never cried. Jess cried at the sappy parts in movies and over birds that had fallen out of their nests, but Lissa reminded us not to touch them, that the parents would reject them if we did even as they flopped around, helpless. Lissa kept tissues in her purse for when we went to the movies so Jess could cry into them.

Lissa was the one who fixed things, not the one who fell apart.

But she did. Lissa cried and the worst thing of all was that I didn't care. I just wanted to get away from her.

So I did. I walked away.

Eight

Jess and Lissa didn't bother to try and talk to me at school anymore after that. They didn't call. One night, a few days after the phone hadn't once rung for me, Mom and Dad asked me about it as the three of us watched television after dinner.

"It's nothing," I said.

"Girl stuff, right?" Mom said, and told me about a fight she'd had back in high school with her best friend until David yelled that he needed help with his homework.

Dad said, "You know, as your mother's boyfriend at the time, I got to hear all about it, so if you ever want a guy's opinion or anything, I'm here."

"Thanks, but I'm fine," I said and watched him smile at me.

Smile, smile, smile, all anyone ever did.

Mom came back, rubbing her head and saying she didn't

remember history being so hard when she was David's age, and every time I looked at them, they were watching me. Grinning at me as I caught their gaze, but when I got up to get a soda, I heard Dad say, "Laura, the letter you sent your parents came back today marked REFUSED again," as I left the room.

My father's parents had died a long time ago, but my mother's parents were still alive. They'd lived in Reardon, but sold their house and moved to a retirement community outside Staunton right before I was born. I'd never met them. They stopped speaking to my mother when she was just a little older than I was. When she told them she was marrying Dad.

When she told them she was pregnant with me.

When I got back to the living room, Mom and Dad stopped talking, their serious expressions wiped clear and replaced by the all-too-familiar smiles. They didn't ask me about Jess and Lissa again, not even as the phone stayed silent.

On Sunday, when we got to church, arriving together in one car like we always did, Jess looked at me and then away, her mouth twisting the way it did when she was upset. I jumped when the organ started to play, startled by the loud buzz of the first note, and suddenly saw a forest all around me, rain-slick and looming.

I wanted to run, but I couldn't. I couldn't move. I didn't think I could breathe.

"Sit down, stupid," David said, and I saw everyone around me was sitting down, ready for prayer. I sat. Mom patted my arm and glared at David. Dad took away the book David was always allowed to read because he found the sermons boring and handed him a Bible.

David grinned at Dad, his I'm-sorry-but-hey-I'm-cute grin. Dad turned away, smiling at Mom and me. I closed my eyes but the forest came back and when I opened them I saw Margaret watching me, squinting so hard the skin between her eyes looked like it was frowning.

After church she cornered me, striding up to me as I was trying to slip outside. "How are you, Meggie?"

"Fine," I said automatically, and she frowned for real then, like she'd heard something she didn't like in my voice.

"You know, when I got back from Vietnam—" she said, and I cut her off, said, "It was nice to see you," and got away, found Mom and told her I didn't want to stay for the covered dish supper.

"Honey, in church you seemed . . . tired," Mom said in the car as she drove me home. "Did you read the paper this morning? Because if you did, you don't have to worry about anything. Those Park Service people certainly do like to complain, as if we all don't know that Staunton's airport is easy enough to get to."

"Right." I hadn't read the paper. I'd seen the headline, *Park Service Officials Predict Problems If Local Airport Closes Permanently*, and immediately pushed it away and asked Dad for the comics.

There weren't as many Park Rangers up in the hills as there used to be because of funding cuts, but there were still a few, and it was because of them that Reardon had an airport. Service had stopped since the crash though, pending an FAA investigation, and I wanted it to stay that way. I didn't want to hear any planes. I definitely didn't want to see any. Just thinking about it made me feel bad, weird and sick.

It's raining really hard, but I can tell we're starting to descend because the trees are closer and the plane is shuddering. It's been bouncing around since we took off, but it's a little plane and that's normal. Totally normal. It is. I look out the window again and the trees are so close, so very close and—

"Meggie?"

I jumped, and Mom put a hand on my arm.

"Sweetie, we're home, and whatever you're thinking about must be good because it was like you weren't in the car at all for a second there." She grinned at me, please-be-all-right-please-you-are-a-miracle shining in that grin and even stronger in her eyes.

I unbuckled my seat belt and got out of the car to get away from her, from everything. Mom waved as she backed down the driveway, returning to church. I waved back even though my arm felt like it was stuck in drying cement.

I couldn't walk up the driveway. I couldn't even move. I knew if I did something horrible would happen. I tried to keep standing, but my knees were shaking so bad I had to sit down.

The driveway was hot. When winter came, it would come hard, but for now the last of summer held on, creating a heat shimmer everywhere I looked. I didn't like that, how everything was blurred around the edges, and stared down at the driveway.

Dad had paved it when David was four, after he'd tried to ride standing up on his kiddie bike and fell, scraping his face and arms on the gravel. Now the driveway was smooth and dark, and the heat of it radiated through the long skirt Mom had brought home for me on Friday, something she'd "grabbed" while out in Derrytown loading up on stuff at the warehouse club. She and Dad hadn't said anything about the weight I'd gained, the way the muscles in my legs had become coated with a soft, shaking layer of fat.

I liked it. I'd always been skinny, so skinny that Dr. Weaver was forever asking Mom if I was eating. When I was born, he'd told her I'd always be sickly and weak, a child to worry over, to keep away from anything strenuous. Then David came along and he was even scrawnier than I was and sickly for real.

But David filled out, became blond and angelic-looking

with soft little dimples of skin around his elbows and knees and chubby little cheeks that he'd never quite lost. I stayed brown-haired and scrawny, but I didn't get sick, and the first time I played soccer I never wanted to stop. I'd stayed totally flat-chested until I was fourteen though, and even then grew just enough to fill an A-cup. I'd hated that, but liked how strong I was, how I could run and kick. I liked feeling my body work.

I didn't want to think about it now. My heart beating. Me breathing. I didn't—I didn't get why any of it was still happening. I felt like it could stop anytime.

I closed my eyes and lay down on the driveway, let the heat of it soak into me. I ran one hand up my side, trying to make sure I was still there, and stopped at my chest. I had actual breasts now, and I poked at the side of one. I completely got why guys loved them now. They were so soft.

"What are you doing?"

I opened my eyes and saw a pair of jean-clad knees down toward the end of the driveway. Up, up, I looked, all the way up to a beautiful, puzzled-looking face. Joe. If I'd known before that all I had to do to get him to talk to me was come home from church and lay down on the driveway on a Sunday afternoon . . .

I never would have done it.

I never was the kind of person who did stuff like that. I was the kind of person who laid out in the backyard wearing a T-shirt over my bathing suit to hide my flat chest and everything else. I was the kind of person who always wore my seat belt, cleaned my room, and did my homework. I was the kind of person who freaked out over pop quizzes or running a mile a tenth of a second slower than usual. I was the kind of person who didn't know what to do when things went wrong.

I was the kind of person who should have died when the plane crashed.

"What does it look like I'm doing?" I was the kind of person who wouldn't have been able to say anything to Joe until long after he'd left.

Was. Now I just didn't care anymore.

"Like you're lying on your driveway feeling yourself up. Did Reverend Williams replace the grape juice with wine at Communion?"

"Nope." I lifted myself onto my elbows, looking at him. "So, you've been standing around watching me?"

"What?" he said, clearly startled, and small stripes of red bloomed on his face, across his cheeks. "I didn't—wasn't—"

"Oh, get over yourself," I said. "So you were watching me. If you came home and lay down on your driveway—with your shirt off, of course—I'd look."

"Like I could lie down on my driveway without your parents seeing and calling the cops. Ever since I got back, it's like they're waiting for me to come over the fence swinging an axe or something."

"Are you?"

He grinned. "I might now."

I started to say something but the wind rustled behind us, pushing through the trees. I couldn't see his smile anymore, just saw red, hungry and waiting, all around me.

I turned around to look at the trees. To see where they were. To make sure they weren't any closer. If I wasn't careful, they'd surround me, scratching me as I moved, waiting to grab me, swallow me—

"Hey, are you all right?" Joe had come up the driveway and was leaning over a little, snapping his fingers next to my face. "Megan?"

The red—the haze—it was fire and it was here. It was inside me. I could feel it hissing, a strange sharp pain that snapped inside my head.

It made me want to scream. It made me want to run.

I pushed myself up and smacked into him, hitting my head on his chin.

"What are—shit!" he said, and took a step back. "I almost bit my tongue off! What the hell is wrong with you? First you go into some sort of trance, then you—Jesus." He brushed the back of his hand across his face. "Crap, I did bite my tongue."

"Trance?"

"You were staring at the—" He gestured back at the trees. "I wasn't sure you were even breathing because you were so still you looked half dea . . ." He trailed off, wiping his mouth again, and I knew, suddenly, what he was thinking about. Who.

And it wasn't me.

"Do you miss Beth?"

He looked at me and then down at the ground, a picture-perfect image of grief, and I was sorry I'd asked. I didn't want posturing, pretending. I'd had enough of that.

Then he said something.

"I don't miss how she went through my stuff," he said, looking up and off into the distance, at something—someone—only he could see, and I saw his grief was real. It was still there, raw inside him. He still missed Beth enough to remember that she wasn't perfect. He still missed her enough to see her as real.

"I don't miss how she was so smart she would say stuff I didn't understand. But I miss the way she got excited about weird stuff like vinegar and would read everything she could about it. She . . . you know, she could have done anything, been anything, but she never got the chance. I hate that she didn't get that like you did."

"Oh. I mean, yes, I got a second chance. I'm very lucky."

He looked at me then. "Yeah?" He didn't sound like he believed a word I said.

I looked back at him and saw I could tell him the truth, or at least part of it. I could tell him, and he'd get it, somehow.

He must have seen that and not wanted any part of it because he turned around and walked away. He didn't say goodbye. He didn't look back.

I didn't feel anything watching him go. I didn't even wish I did.

Nine

There were four people on the plane with me. Carl, casting glances at my pretzels and telling stories. Walter, tugging at his hat and talking excitedly about trees. Sandra, arms cut with muscles that flexed whenever she moved, fiddling with her seat belt and jiggling one leg. Henry, with his weathered face and brown hair combed flat with dandruff flaking in his part.

Four people, all gone.

And then I started to see them.

When I went outside to my car one morning, Carl was standing by it, Sandra and Walter just behind him.

"Missed a chance to grab lunch earlier," Carl said. "Why is it that there aren't any vending machines in airports? Seems like it would be a great place to put them."

"Stop it," I said. "This isn't real. You're—you aren't here."

Mom tapped the kitchen window, waving at me and mouthing, "Did you forget something?"

I forced myself to wave back, to shake my head.

Walter cleared his throat and said, "When my sister went to Japan, she said there were vending machines everywhere."

Carl shot him a look. "Japan? Who the hell is talking about Japan? You're not from around here, are you?"

"No." Walter flushed and tugged on his hat.

"Look, I just want to get home," Sandra said. "My daughter's been sick, and now my husband's got her cold, and I hate flying and just want to get this over with." She raised her voice a little, and looked at me. "Why are we waiting here?"

I got in the car then. I backed down the driveway. I didn't look back to see if Sandra and Carl and Walter were still there. Still waiting.

I'd been there during that conversation. It was . . . it had happened. It was real and I could remember all of it now. We'd been in Staunton, waiting for the plane. I could see the thin blue airport carpet, scuffed with shoe prints. Sandra had turned away when I'd shrugged after she'd asked why we were waiting, looked out the airport window. There had been nothing to see except asphalt and then, past that, a drainage ditch and a fence. We couldn't even see our plane.

I drove to school, my hands wet and shaking on the steering

wheel, and told myself it was just a memory. That's all it was. They weren't real. They weren't here.

But they were, and after that first time, I couldn't get rid of them. Couldn't stop seeing them. When the sun rose, I would peer out my bedroom window and see them sitting on the lawn waiting for me. On the way to school, I'd see Carl cracking his knuckles. Walter would be at school, in the halls tugging nervously on his hat. Sandra would be in the kitchen when I got home, reading the little airline safety booklet and frowning.

They were dead. I knew that. But I saw them anyway, and I felt something when I saw them.

I was scared, and I didn't like that.

I didn't like that at all.

I would close my eyes when I saw them, tell myself I could make them go away. That they were just in my mind.

But when I opened my eyes, they were always still there.

School got harder. I couldn't concentrate, my mind gritty with exhaustion and fear. And then Coach Henson asked me to come back to soccer. "Team needs you, Megan," he said when I came into school one morning. "Needs your skills. Your strength. You'll come to practice today, won't you?"

"I—" I said, and beside him Henry shook his head, dandruff snowing from his hair, and waved at Carl, who was standing right beside me.

"Can get bumpy up in the hills," Henry said. "Is all that damned luggage yours?"

I nodded, terrified.

"Fantastic," Coach said. "I knew I could count on you."

"Don't mind Henry," Carl said. "It won't hurt him to deal with a suitcase or two. Say, you don't have anything to eat on you, do you?"

Henry wasn't there. Carl wasn't there. I wasn't really seeing them. *I wasn't.* I watched Coach smile and told myself I had to try and be the Megan I was supposed to be.

So I tried. When classes were over I went down to the practice field. I didn't see Carl or Sandra or Walter or Henry anywhere. Maybe it would be okay. Maybe I really could play soccer again.

We ran first. Warming up, Coach yelling encouragement and telling us to move. My body felt strange, not light and in danger of floating away like it usually did. Instead, I felt awkward, slow. Weighed down. My lungs hurt, and I couldn't get into an easy rhythm.

I kept going, though, and toward the end of the last loop around the field, I felt something inside me relax. I felt my body moving, saw the last curve of the field, the patch of grass where we always stopped. It was dented and yellowed from where everyone stood, sweating and ready to play, and when I finally got there, my lungs were on fire and my whole body hurt. The muscles in my legs were trembling, and sweat was pouring down my face. But I felt good. I felt connected to myself in a way I hadn't since I'd opened my eyes and found out I was a miracle.

I felt real.

Then I saw the soccer balls. Coach tipped them out, pointing and yelling as he kicked one to each of us. "Stacey, get over there! Kathleen, hustle! Megan, let's focus on the attack! Wait a minute, what's with your shoes?"

I hadn't worn my cleats. They were still on the roof. And when the soccer ball came toward me, black and white circling round and round, everything got dark, my vision narrowing like I was going to faint.

I staggered back a step, the ground a pinpoint I could hardly see, the sky a speck of fading blue that seemed wrong. False. I knew what was really there. What was underneath.

I knew that past the blue was smoke and flames and the burning sky; the hidden one, real one, would crackle red and wrap itself around me. I saw pieces of clothing and shoes and a soccer ball melting together, burning as a hand touched mine, its skin cracking and blistering and—

I bit the inside of my cheek as hard as I could. It hurt, and blood filled my mouth, the world coming back as I spit, watched red spatter the ground.

I backed away from the soccer balls, from the field. I backed up until everything was a blur, Coach's questions a buzz in my ears, and then I went home.

When I got there, I went in the bathroom. I put two fingers in the left side of my mouth, stretching it wide as I stared at myself in the mirror. There was a raw red spot inside my mouth. It hurt when I touched it. I pulled my fingers free and watched my face settle back into place, blank and pale except for the dark circles under my eyes.

I had been here before. I stared in the mirror and saw rain falling all around me, felt it slapping my hair, my face, and my feet.

I'm cold and tired and my head hurts and I saw—I trip over something, a tree, a rock, my own feet, and I don't mind that I will hit the ground. I would like to close my eyes. But my mouth, which is open, panting, snaps shut and my teeth catch on skin, tearing. I spit, red more red, and the wind blows through the trees, pushing me forward, and I go, one foot in front of the other in front of the other in front of the other because I know what is behind me and I don't want to see it.

I left the bathroom. I went to my room, shut the door, and opened the window.

Up on the roof, I could feel the sun hot on the bottoms of my feet, burning through my shoes. The ground looked far away. The trees didn't. Around me were my soccer shoes, the afghan I'd gotten, and the clothes I'd been wearing when the plane crashed, the ones Mom and Dad had saved in a bag I wasn't ever going to open again.

I looked down at the ground. I had fallen into it before. Maybe I should have stayed there. I leaned over more, closer.

Carl stared up at me, mouth open and hands reaching toward me. His face was bloody, melting.

I almost lost my balance and felt my heart hammer in my chest as I slipped to my knees, my hands scrabbling over the hot roof as I tried to steady myself.

David got off the bus and walked through Carl on his way to the house. I blinked hard, wiping my eyes with one hand.

Carl was gone; I just saw ground now. I climbed back into my room and shut the window, then closed the curtains.

At dinner, I told Mom and Dad I wasn't ever going to play soccer again.

Dad opened his mouth, shocked-looking, but Mom put a hand on top of one of his and he closed it.

"Are you—are you sure about this?" Mom said, and then bit her lip like she'd said something she shouldn't have.

"I'm sure," I said, and she smiled but I knew she'd almost asked me something else. Almost asked me if I was all right. If anything was wrong. But she hadn't.

She hadn't, Dad hadn't, and they weren't going to. I was a

miracle, and they needed that. I didn't know why, but I could see it in how they looked at me. In all the things they didn't say.

"I got an A on my math test," David said.

Once upon a time Mom and Dad would have made him get his test and stuck it on the fridge. They would have told him how proud they were. Once upon a time they looked at him and saw proof of a special gift they'd been given, a baby who hadn't been expected to live but had. A miracle.

No one said anything to David now.

"I hate you," he told me before he went to bed, opening my bedroom door and hissing the words at me. "Mom and Dad act like you're perfect, but everyone else knows you're crazy."

"No," I said. "You're the only one who does."

David looked surprised, and then he made a face at me and slammed my door.

Dad called out, "Meggie, are you all right?"

I got up and opened my door. David was standing at the top of the stairs, looking down into the living room where Mom and Dad sat. He looked so lost, so hurt.

"I'm fine," I said, and shut my bedroom door so I wouldn't see him cry.

Ten

Jess was waiting at my locker after second period the next morning. I ducked into the bathroom and locked myself in a stall. I heard her come in, saw her feet pause by the stall door as the bell rang, but I knew Jess. She could never be late for class. She'd be gone when I opened the door.

She was, but there was a note shoved into my locker, Jess's round handwriting sprawled across a piece of notebook paper. *Call me. Please.*

I crumpled the note, watching the words disappear, and then, instead of going to class or even the library, I went home.

Mom showed up about an hour later, tires screeching as her car flew up the driveway, and she stayed home with me for the rest of the day. She felt my forehead constantly, said she'd heard there was a bad cold going around. She said I needed to rest. We watched her soap opera and made cookies.

She asked me how I felt, but she never asked what I was thinking. I think she hoped that the food and the attention, the constant kindness, would make me into the girl I was supposed to be.

But that girl could never be—not ever—and so that night, I ran.

I was in bed, wrapped up in my covers with my hands resting on my belly so I could feel myself breathing. My eyes were gritty as I waited for sleep, only to have it come for moments. I was waking up with a start as soon as dreams came for me, trying to take me somewhere I knew I didn't want to go.

I lay there and remembered running at soccer practice, remembered how I had been able to just focus on it. How, for a little while, I had felt like I was really here. I got up, got dressed, climbed out my window, and slid down onto the porch. From there I dropped onto the grass, and then I ran.

I ran down our driveway, our street. The trees were dark shadows, like everything else, and I ran past them, too busy hearing myself breathing, too busy feeling my body working slowly, clumsily.

I ran until I couldn't anymore. I didn't get very far.

I had to walk back because I'd overdone it. I could feel my hamstrings tightening in protest already and when I got back to the house I stood on the driveway for a second, looking up at the porch.

Looking up at my room waiting for me, looking at the open window leading to my bed, leading to me lying there awake and waiting for another day I didn't want.

I climbed up anyway, feeling my arms shake as I pushed myself onto the roof.

"What are you doing?"

I looked around and saw Joe leaning out his bedroom window watching me.

"What does it look like?"

He grinned. I could see what looked liked a hickey on his neck, a dark spot on his pale skin, and his hair was sticking up in the back, like someone had been running their fingers through it. "Did you lock yourself out?"

"No."

I was sliding one foot toward my window when he spoke again. "Then what are you doing?"

I glanced over at his window. He'd leaned out of it far enough so I could still see him, head tilted to one side as he watched me.

"Not what you're doing."

He grinned again, wider, and touched the hickey. "What, this? I got it earlier. Believe me, if I had a girl in my room right now, I wouldn't be watching you try to break your neck."

I froze halfway through my window, my arms burning as I held myself still. "I'm not trying to break my neck."

"You wouldn't anyway. You're not up high enough. You'd just mess up your mother's flowerbeds and maybe break your arm."

"How do you know?"

"Because Beth saw your brother jump off the roof the time he made a parachute," he said. "And when he was in the hospital getting his arm set, she calculated that it would be almost impossible to die jumping off your roof. She wanted to put that in the get-well card she made, but Mom talked her out of it. She said 'Feel Better' was nicer than math problems about death."

"I'd forgotten all about David and the roof," I said. "I bet he might still have the card Beth—"

"I haven't forgotten," he said, and I heard his window close. I slid inside mine, shaking my arms out and wondering what Joe had seen in my face to make him say what he had.

I pushed the thought away and went back to bed, hoping that now I could sleep.

I didn't.

Eleven

I got to school late the next morning and was greeted by the sight of Coach Henson standing in the parking lot, arms folded across his chest as he paced back and forth like it was game day. Maybe it was. I didn't know the team schedule anymore.

He waved me down as soon as I got out of the car like he'd been waiting for me.

"Talked to a few of your teachers the other day," he said. "Seems you've had trouble keeping up with your schoolwork. Also, your guidance counselor says you're behind on your independent study. You were supposed to turn in your outline and a general thesis statement last week, remember?"

I shrugged.

"Look, normally I wouldn't say anything but—" He broke off, sighed, and then cleared his throat like he always did before he said something he thought was important. "I know classes can be boring sometimes, but that's how classes are, right? And everyone—and I mean everyone—is impressed by how courageous you are. But you need to keep applying yourself, because if you don't—well, if you don't, you're going to be letting yourself down. And I know you don't want that."

I stared at him. He smiled at me. I didn't smile back.

"Well," he said, "I know you'll power through. And look, I'll take care of your late slip, so you just get over to the auditorium with everyone else."

"Auditorium?"

He nodded. "Senior portraits, remember? Now go on, and think about what I said."

Things only got worse from there.

The auditorium was so crowded, people packed together everywhere. In the aisles, by the doors, and it was hot too, everyone crowded together, so close and I—I dug my nails into my palms trying to steady myself. It didn't work.

I had to get out of there, but when I turned around there were already people behind me, leaning against the doors I'd just come through. Behind their heads I could see the tiny windows at the tops of the doors, high enough to offer only a view of the hallway ceiling, of empty space.

Airplane windows were about that size, and people pressed up against them too, looking out into nothing.

I headed toward the exit at the far side of the auditorium, my legs shaking so badly I thought I was going to fall down. I tried not to look at anyone but I saw Jess and Lissa sitting together. Jess said something and Lissa laughed, doubling over the way she did when she got caught up in a giggling fit. Jess laughed too and then hugged Lissa. Her eyes caught mine as she did, and her smile slipped.

I looked away and kept walking. It was hard to get past the seemingly endless rows of seats, so close together they could have been on a plane. I looked at the floor, trying not to think about that, but when I looked up everyone had vanished and there was nothing to see but row after row of empty chairs. It was only for a second but my heart started beating so hard I could actually feel it fluttering in my chest. I ran the last few steps to the door and pushed it open.

Outside, I sat down, curled up tight with my arms around my legs and my head pressed into my knees until I could breathe again.

There was no way I could drive home. Just walking by the lot and seeing my car made me feel sick. So I walked, but between the road and the trees and myself, I felt worse and worse with every step I took, shaky and light-headed, hollowed out. I started to be afraid that if I took another step I'd die or vanish or, worse, realize I was somewhere else, like on a plane . . .

I dug my nails into my palms again to force myself to keep walking and, after a while, realized I was by the church. Reverend Williams's car was parked by the office that had been built off to the side. Margaret's car was next to it.

It was cool inside the church, and dark. No trees. No road. The pews looked like pews and not airline seats, and I sat down.

"Aren't you supposed to be in school?"

Margaret was behind me, carrying a bunch of flowers for the vases up by the altar. I shrugged, not wanting to talk to her, but not ready to get up and leave either.

"Well, don't just sit there. Come give me a hand with these flowers."

So I helped Margaret arrange the flowers. She didn't talk much, except to say things like, "Taller ones in the back, please," or "You've got too much greenery on the right side. Pull some out. No, your other right side."

"Good enough," she said after she decided we were done, pushing her glasses up with one finger and squinting at the flowers. She looked over at me. "Didn't see that car of yours out front."

"Didn't drive it."

"I see." I didn't like the way her voice sounded, like she knew something about me.

I shrugged and told myself not to look away from her. It was surprisingly hard.

"You know, you look terrible," she said. "Hard to tell where those circles under your eyes end and you begin. Come on, I'll fix you lunch and then take you home."

Why were old people able to get away with being so rude? "I'll walk, thank you."

"All right," she said, and turned back to the flowers, re-arranging them again.

I left, but outside I only made it to the edge of the parking lot before I had to stop. I didn't feel like I had before, sick and frightened. I just felt trapped. Where could I go? Back to school and my car? And then what? Home, where I'd lie around trying not to see things that weren't there, where I had to act like everything was fine, like I was a miracle?

I *was* trapped, and realizing that made me want to throw things. To reach up and grab hold of the sky with both hands and pull, rip the world apart.

"You can't stand here all day, you know," Margaret said from behind me, and touched my shoulder.

I jumped; I couldn't help it, and stepped away from her. She took a step back herself, and flinched at the look on my face. It was strange to see someone so old do that. Wrong, somehow.

"I'm going to walk home and make some lunch," she said. "You can come if you want."

I went. Not because I wanted to, or even because it was something to do before I went back to the inevitable and waited through the rest of the day.

I went because she flinched. Because when she looked at me, she clearly didn't see a miracle. She saw something the opposite of that, something lost and broken.

I went because she saw me.

I'd never been to her house, not even when Rose was alive and they sometimes invited people to come back across the street for coffee after church. Inside, it was smaller than I'd thought and ruthlessly clean. "Leave your shoes there," Margaret said as soon as I walked in, and pointed at a neat row of them by the door. I recognized one pair. Rose had a pair of bright blue clogs she'd worn in the summer and I put mine as far away from them as I could. It wasn't that I didn't like Rose or anything like that. It just seemed like a good idea to stay away from dead people's things.

I already had enough dead people around me.

"Sit down," Margaret said when I came into the kitchen, and then gave me a glass of milk.

"I don't like milk."

"Everyone likes milk."

"I don't."

"Drink it anyway. I have to take a pill once a week to help my bones and it's all because I never drank enough milk."

I took a sip. It was skim, not the 2% Mom bought, and it tasted like water. When I was a kid I'd sometimes wondered what it would be like to have a grandmother. Now I knew I wasn't missing anything.

Margaret opened a cabinet and got out some bread and a can of something. "You know, it was very pretty over in Vietnam. Not during the fighting, of course, and certainly not after, but sometimes when I'm talking about the war, or even when I think about everything that happened, I'll remember that, how pretty the land was. I don't think I noticed it more than once or twice, really, but it's stayed with me all these years."

She opened another cabinet and got out two plates. "Rose didn't agree with me, and after a couple of fights, I just stopped trying to explain how I felt to her." She glanced at me. "You want mayo?"

I shook my head. She was making deviled ham; I'd smelled it as soon as she'd opened the can, and I only liked ham with mustard on it. I didn't know what to think about what she'd just told me. I didn't know much about Vietnam and I didn't know what her story meant.

I guess she could tell because she stopped making sandwiches long enough to squint at me. "When we got back, I couldn't stand loud noises. Reminded me of things I didn't want to remember. So I made myself walk by Derek Ginty's house back when he got his first car—this was well before you were even born—and listened to it backfire when he was trying to work on it. I used to end up standing there looking like you did today. And Rose . . . it was different for her. She couldn't stand hospitals. The thought of all the sick people inside, all their suffering, it—it got to her. So she stayed away from them, and wouldn't hardly ever even go to see a doctor. She had a hard time going to LaMotte, even when it was toward the end. A bitter, hard time."

She put a sandwich in front of me. "Do you understand what I'm saying?"

I stared at her and my throat felt tight, like there were things—words—trapped in it.

"I should go wash up," I said, and pushed away from the table.

"Down the hall on the left," Margaret said. "And don't use the soaps in the little basket. Or touch the green towels."

The bathroom, small and painted a pale green, was right across from a bedroom. The door to it was closed, and I figured it had been Rose's. I washed my hands and dried them off on the little green towels I wasn't supposed to use, glancing at the other door in the bathroom, the one that led into Margaret's room.

I fiddled with the door that led back out into the hallway, and then looked at the other one. I couldn't help but wonder what Margaret's room was like. I bet everything was arranged according to size or alphabetically, something like that. I didn't know how Rose had put up with her, best friend or not, for all those years.

But the room wasn't Margaret's. It was Rose's. I could tell as soon as I opened the door. The walls were a sunny yellow, the bed had a bright homemade quilt on it, and a couple of the bears she'd made for every kid in church the Christmas I was seven were on a dresser, the ones that hadn't been taken because some of the parents wouldn't let their kids have them. There were some pictures too, but I wasn't close enough to see them and I didn't feel right walking around the room.

I saw a pair of Margaret's glasses next to one of the pictures, like she'd come in to look around and had to leave in a hurry. I guess she didn't feel right in here either. That was sad.

I went back into the bathroom and headed into the hallway. I didn't feel bad about peeking in the other room now, especially since I'd already accidentally seen Rose's. Plus I really wasn't in a hurry to go back out to my sandwich and Margaret. I'd wanted someone to understand how I felt, but I wasn't so sure I wanted that someone to be Margaret.

I opened the other door.

It wasn't Margaret's room. It wasn't a bedroom at all. It was a study or something, a desk with an old computer in one corner, and a bunch of bookshelves along the walls. There was a comfy-looking sofa in the other corner, two more of Rose's teddy bears sitting on top of it. One of them was wearing glasses perched halfway down its nose, and the other one was wearing a pink sweatshirt that said SILVER FOX. They were holding hands.

I don't know how long I stood there before I figured it out. Before I got that those bears were supposed to be Margaret and Rose. Before I knew that I could look in every other room in the house and never find another bedroom.

"Meggie, what on earth are you still doing in the bath . . . ?" Margaret's voice, loud at first, trailed off altogether. I could feel her looking at me, at the room, at the bears sitting together, and then back at me.

"You didn't know." She sounded surprised. I guess she should have been. I'd always wondered why some people in town and even at church wouldn't talk to them, why Jess's mother had glanced at mine and muttered, "Let's hope not," the time I said, "Me and Jess are going to be friends forever just like Margaret and Rose," after we got drunk on peach schnapps we snuck during her aunt's bachelorette party.

"No," I said. "I didn't."

"Well, you do now. You want me to drive you home, or do you want to walk?" Margaret's voice was crisp but when I looked over at her she was staring at the bears with a sad look on her face, like she'd had this conversation before. Like people looked at her after they knew and stopped seeing her.

"Can I have my sandwich first?"

She glanced at me. She didn't smile. She frowned, then squinted at me, and after a long while she nodded.

So I ate my sandwich, and then she drove me home. "Tell your parents you were at my house," she said when I got out of the car. "I don't want them hearing from someone else."

"They won't care."

"Tell them anyway," Margaret said.

Twelve

"It's a nice surprise to see you here and not up in your room," Mom said as she came into the living room. I was sitting on the sofa watching a bunch of news guys yell at each other about taxes. It was just like a talk show except everyone was wearing ties. "Want a snack?"

"Nah. I'm still kind of full from lunch."

"What did you have?" She sat down next to me.

"Ham. Margaret made it. Well, not the ham. The sandwiches."

"Margaret? From church?"

"Yep."

"You . . . you ate lunch with her? At her house?"

I nodded.

"Well. That's . . . did you have a nice time?"

"Sure. Have you ever been to her house?" I already knew

the answer. One of the guys on TV was yelling so loud his face was bright red.

"No," Mom said, and her voice had gone high and sort of strangled sounding. "Is it nice?"

"Small. One bathroom. One bedroom."

She got off the sofa. "I didn't see your car in the driveway. Did it break down?"

"No, it's at school."

"I'll call your father and have him go look at it," she said, and went into the kitchen. I could have heard what she said to Dad if I'd turned the television down, but I could already guess what it was.

Dad came home about ten minutes later. He stopped in the kitchen, saying something to Mom I didn't try to listen to, and then came into the living room. "What happened to the car?"

"Nothing. I just didn't want to drive home. Can you give me a ride to school in the morning?"

"Sure. I'd like to take a look at it though, just in case. And—well, your mother says . . . she tells me you had lunch with Margaret."

I nodded. "I ran into her at church."

"At church?"

"Yeah."

"What were you doing there?"

I shrugged.

He cleared his throat and then kissed the top of my head. "Praying isn't anything to be shy about, Meggie. And as for Margaret, I think she's been lonely since Rose died, and I'm sure it did her good to talk. It was a nice thing you did, and if you want to do it again, it's fine with me."

"George!" Mom called from the kitchen.

"I don't see what the big deal is," Dad called back. "Meggie had lunch with someone from church. Someone we've known for years. Someone who has only had kind things to say to us, even back when we first got married." He turned to me. "What did you have to eat?"

"Deviled ham."

He made a face. Dad hated ham. "Well, then it was definitely very nice of you."

"George!" Mom said again, and Dad squeezed my shoulder. "I'll let you get back to your show now."

When he went back into the kitchen, I turned the television down.

"That's it?" I heard Mom say. "That's all you have to say?"

"Let's see. Margaret made her lunch. I don't see what the problem is."

"You know I like Margaret. But I just . . . I know what the Bible says."

"I know what the Bible says too," Dad said, sounding tired. "'Let him without sin cast the first stone.' And while you may feel up to it, Laura, I know I don't."

"George—"

"Do you remember the look on your father's face when you told him you were pregnant and I said we were getting married? I do. Do you remember their silence when Meggie was born, or when it looked like David . . . when it looked like he wouldn't make it? Even when the news about Meggie's plane came out, nothing. They've never said a word to us through everything, and all those letters you write come back unopened. We've been judged by others for what you and I have done, by family even, and I won't do that to someone else. Only God should have that right."

Mom sniffed twice, and then said, "George," again, her voice cracking. I turned the television back up.

She came up to my room that night, before I was supposed to go to sleep. She kissed me good night and then took my hands in hers. "I think what you did for Margaret today was awfully kind, and I don't want you to think that I don't love you or don't see how wonderful you are, all right?"

I nodded, fiddling with the top of her wedding ring. It winked up at me, glinting as she flicked off my lamp and threw my room into darkness. I lay there, staring at the ceiling and sure I wouldn't fall asleep.

And then I did.

I woke up under a burning sky, my whole body aching, my mouth full of smoke, and when I looked down I saw green and brown disappearing under the smoke, under flames falling from the sky. I saw a snake moving across the ground, pushing awkwardly on its belly, its yellow scales a blur. The snake twitched, then screamed, and I realized it wasn't a snake but a woman. Her hair was on fire and her hands were clawing at the ground, a gold ring on one finger flashing in the flames.

I woke up shaking, my mouth open but my throat closed up so tight my scream was a silent one, stayed inside me. I woke up and lay there, unable to push the dream away. I woke up and knew the woman from my dream was Sandra.

Sandra, from Flight 619. Sandra, with a baby that she'd left behind.

I woke up and knew what I'd dreamed wasn't a dream at all.

I stayed home from school that day. My head hurt, a sharp band of pain across my forehead and behind my eyes. I told Mom and regretted it right away when she knelt down beside me, anxiety on her face as she felt my forehead and then yelled at Dad to call the doctor.

"I've just got a headache," I told her. "It's not a big deal. I'll get up. I'm fine." But it was too late, and I knew I was going to have to spend the morning in Dr. Weaver's office.

I couldn't stop thinking about my dream, about Sandra clawing at the ground. I shouldn't have survived that. I shouldn't have been able to walk away. Not when . . . Sandra had burned to death. Screaming, in pain, and I'd—

I put my head in my hands.

"Meggie, what's wrong?" Mom sounded frantic, at the edge of tears, and I lifted my head. She relaxed, a sigh pushing out of her, and when I came downstairs because she'd been—of course—able to get an appointment with Dr. Weaver, she put a plate of food in front of me. I ate it fast and asked for more. When my stomach started hurting I was able to stop thinking.

When I saw him, Dr. Weaver took a look at me and said I seemed run down. He wanted me to go to the emergency clinic and have some blood drawn for tests.

"Now, I know how that sounds, but it's just a precaution and our lab is closed today, otherwise I'd do it here," he said, and I watched Mom bite her lip before she nodded.

"Laura, it's all right. You've got two wonderful kids. You're very lucky. You shouldn't worry so much."

"But Meggie said she had a headache," Mom whispered, and there were tears in her eyes. "And when I went into her room she was just lying there staring at the ceiling and all I could think . . ." She broke off, pressing one hand to her mouth. I could see her fingers shaking.

Dr. Weaver patted her on the shoulder. "Frankly, I'm more worried about you than Meggie. I haven't seen you this upset since David was just a little thing. I know what you went through when you thought Meggie was gone. But children have headaches and stomachaches and it's perfectly normal. Meggie is perfectly normal."

I stared at him (*perfectly normal?*) as he flipped through papers in the folder he was holding. "One last look at what I've got here before you both go, all right? Let's see . . . temperature's normal, pulse is fine, and Megan measured half an inch over five-four, which is a little taller than when we measured her last year. Ah, and she's up to one hundred twelve pounds—twelve more than last year. That's very good. Now, I suspect the headache is just a headache, but we'll run those tests just to make absolutely sure. In the meantime, it can never hurt to get plenty of rest and lots of fluids." And that was it. He was done and gone, leaving us with a quick good-bye.

Walter was sitting in the waiting room when I came out with Mom, fiddling with his hat. I wasn't surprised to see him but then he followed us outside. That did surprise me, and my head, which had started to feel a little better, began to hurt again. I closed my eyes and told myself he wasn't there, but he even followed us into the car.

On our way to the clinic he was in the backseat, just sitting there, waiting, every time I turned around.

"Sweetie, are you looking for something?" Mom asked as we pulled into the clinic parking lot.

"No," I said, and watched Walter fiddle with his hat, knowing he wasn't really there but unable to stop seeing him.

He didn't follow us inside, and when the doors clicked closed behind us, I let out a breath I didn't know I was holding and wiped my sweating, shaking hands on my jeans.

"You know," Mom said a minute or two after we'd sat down to wait, "it feels strange to be here without David, doesn't it? Remember the Fourth of July when he stepped on the rake?"

I nodded, staring at the television bolted to the wall because I was afraid of what I'd see if I looked anywhere else.

"Laura, is that you?" The lab tech, Jackie, poked her head into the waiting room. "It is! I thought I heard you. Wait, where's David?"

Mom laughed. "He isn't here today! I was just talking about it with Meggie, actually. How's Dan doing? How are you doing?" She got up and went over to her and within seconds the two of them had started talking about everything from how their hair looked to things they'd done back in high school. They disappeared back into the clinic, but a second later Mom came out and waved at me to follow.

"Hey there, Meggie," Jackie said, opening up a lab cabinet. "Let me get everything ready. Laura, how's work going? Dan wants one of those new lawn tractors and is convinced we'd be able to get credit for trading in the old one. I told him he was crazy. He is crazy, right? Meggie, just have a seat in the chair and hold an arm out for me."

I couldn't do it. Walter was back. He was sitting in the chair I was supposed to, still fiddling with his hat. On the wall behind him I saw a plane window, cracked open with a piece of rock shoved through it. There was blood everywhere, dripping, and below it—

"Go on, have a seat," Jackie said again. She was standing next to Walter now and he looked up at me, waiting.

"I—I can't," I said, and fled into the hall.

Mom came out too, confused and then alarmed at whatever she saw on my face. "Oh, Meggie, sweetie, sit down." She helped me slide down the wall to the floor.

"Looks like someone's a little woozy," Jackie said, coming into the hall as well and kneeling in front of me. "Are you afraid of needles?" When I didn't say anything she looked over at Mom, who was staring worriedly at me.

Walter came out into the hallway then. He sat down right across from me, still turning his hat around and around in his hands. I didn't want to see that anymore. I didn't want to see him anymore. I didn't want to see anything. I closed my eyes.

Mom touched my forehead. "Meggie, what's wrong?" She leaned in closer. I could feel her breath on my face, smell her perfume. "Megan?" Her voice was high and frightened.

I opened my eyes. Walter was still sitting on the floor across from me but now Sandra was next to him too, head bowed so I couldn't see her face, and for a second I saw her as she'd been in my dream, slithering across the ground, green-brown ground burning underneath and all around her.

I stood up so fast my head swam, spots dancing in front of my eyes.

"Careful there," Jackie said, patting my arm. I jumped away, but she acted like she didn't notice, turned to Mom and said, "She's probably got a migraine. My sister gets them all the time. Pain like you wouldn't believe and the awful lights they have in here don't help. You know I love Doc Weaver, but Meggie doesn't need tests. She needs to go home and straight to bed. Anybody can tell just by looking at her that she's fine. I mean, a plane crash couldn't even stop her."

"That's true," Mom said, smiling now. "Meggie is a—"

I stopped listening because I knew what she was going to say. I knew what word she would use to mean me.

And I knew I was anything but that.

Thirteen

The next day I waited.

I waited in my room, in the dark, for the sun to come up. I waited for homemade waffles for breakfast. I waited while David claimed his leg hurt, limping to the front door, and Dad said, "David, no one has time for this. Please stop acting like your leg is going to fall off and go wait for the bus. I need to take Meggie to school."

"Everything's always about Megan," David said, then glared at me and slammed the front door as he left.

At school, I waited while Dad checked my car to make sure it was running okay.

"It's fine," he said, and I waited while he hugged me good-bye and drove off.

In school, I waited for every class to end. I drew squares

and circles in my notebook. I took a test in French, leaving blank spaces for my answers and flipping the paper over instead. I drew a map of the school, the cafeteria at the center with four enclosed hallways branching off at each corner, one outside hallway connecting them all. A square within a square, I thought, and drew in all the doors. I knew where every exit was.

I erased the map before I turned the test in.

On the drive home I waited to float up out of my body or for Walter or Carl or Sandra or Henry to show up in the passenger seat.

Nothing happened.

At home, I ate fish-shaped cheese crackers while lying on the kitchen floor. From where I was, the happy ducks on Mom's dish towels were upside down, their dancing feet looking more like they were flailing, trying to find somewhere to land.

When I got tired of looking at them I sat at the kitchen table and waited for David to come home. I left the kitchen when he came in. We didn't say anything to each other. I'd waited for that too.

At night, David ran into the bathroom just when I was getting ready to go in and brush my teeth, laughing as he locked the door.

I opened it—the door only had a button lock, and it would pop if you pushed the handle down hard enough.

He glared at me when I walked in. I ignored him and picked up my toothbrush.

"Give me the toothpaste," I said.

"No. I'm using it." He was loud, and we both heard Mom get up, heard her footsteps on the stairs.

He grinned at me, all teeth, and then yelled, "Ow! Meggie, don't hit me!"

I stared at him, at his open mouth, his angry eyes, and then leaned toward him, putting my free hand on the back of his neck. I could see both of us in the mirror over the sink.

"Shut up," I said quietly, not moving, but what I really wanted to do was smash his face into the sink, have Mom walk in and see me doing it, see my face as it looked right now.

David stared at me in the mirror, his eyes wide and afraid, and then broke away from me and ran out of the room, his toothbrush and the toothpaste hitting the floor.

"David Jacob," I heard Mom say out in the hallway, and then, "David, come back here!"

"What happened?" she said to me, coming into the bathroom. "Did you two fight?"

I shrugged and she turned away, went into David's room. I could hear him crying when she opened his door.

She came back into the bathroom when I was rinsing my mouth out. "He says you told him to shut up."

I spit into the sink and waited. Now something would happen. I knew David would tell Mom what I'd done.

I knew he'd tell her what he'd seen when he looked at me.

"Meggie, I know he wants attention and that it can be hard, but no matter how much he tries to upset you, I'd really appreciate it if you didn't . . . you shouldn't say things like 'shut up.' It's just not nice."

I stared at her in the mirror. She was fiddling with the ends of my hair, tucking them under so the lengths matched. "We should drive up to Derrytown and get your hair trimmed. Would you like that?"

She didn't look at me as she said it, and I knew she wasn't going to say anything else. She knew something had happened, that David had seen something in me, something messed up, broken, and she didn't want to know what it was. She didn't want to see it.

She wouldn't see it.

I had to get away from her then. I put my toothbrush down and moved past her, walking downstairs. I yanked open the front door, the night air warm on my face.

"Sweetie," she said, running after me, and for a second I felt something hopeful flare inside me. I turned toward her.

"Here," she said, and handed me my sneakers and a pair of socks. "You can't go out barefoot. And don't come home too late, okay? You know how your father worries."

That was it. That was all she said. It was night, I was going running again, and she—I yanked the shoes away from her and left.

I ran. I put on my shoes in the driveway and then flew down it. The trees were nothing to me now, just dark shadows, and what was a shadow?

Nothing; it was nothing and I'd known my parents wanted the crash to have left me whole, wanted to believe I was fine. That it had even somehow made me special.

I'd never thought that if they knew something was definitely wrong with me, in me, they'd pretend it away.

But that's what had happened. What was happening.

I ran all the way to the center of town and then out past it, pushing one hand against my side to try and stop the stitch that had formed there.

It didn't work and I ended up having to stop, panting. My side hurt bad, and my lungs felt like they were on fire. Reardon didn't have much in the way of streetlights, and there were only faint pools of light coming from people's houses, tiny half-moons on their lawns that didn't quite reach me. I kept waiting for the dark to bother me, for the sound of the wind blowing softly through the trees to break me.

It didn't happen. I liked being in the dark. I liked not

being seen. I walked and walked, ended up on the edge of the road that circled around town, running from the hills behind Reardon Logging's offices into town and then back up into the hills on the other side, leading to the Park Service offices. And the airport.

I kicked at some loose gravel on the side of the road, and then moved to avoid a truck coming around the corner. It was Mr. Reynolds's. I could tell just by the sound. When he got a job driving tractor trailers, the first thing he did was buy a new truck and fiddle with the muffler so that every time he turned the engine over you could hear it all the way down the street. Supposedly he spent a lot of time driving by his ex-wife's boy-friend's place for a while.

After he passed, I started jogging back toward town. Mr. Reynolds must have been to see Beth because he only ever did two things when he was home. He either sat in his house and drank, or he drove up to Beth's grave and drank. Her grave was in the town cemetery, which was up the road from where I was when the truck had passed me.

It was like death was everywhere I went. I shivered and stopped jogging. I wasn't even back in town yet, but I just—I didn't feel like going anywhere. I was standing in what every-one called the fire zone, a gap that circled Reardon, serving as a buffer between the town and the forest. Reardon had been built that way because the settlers that first came here were from another logging community, and they'd lost everything when a fire set to clear some of the forest ended up destroying their town. It had been called Reardon too.

I would have sat down, but the road out here was just gravel and there was no grass beside it, nothing but dirt and prickly weeds. It was a nowhere place and I liked that, stood there because it felt like it was where I belonged.

Fourteen

I don't know how long I stood there, in that nowhere place. Long enough for the dark around me to get deeper and quieter, the faint, far-off light from houses in town disappearing as people ended their day. Long enough for Mr. Reynolds's pickup to drive by again, its big headlights catching me as it passed. I moved back but it was too late. The truck slowed down, pulling off the road and onto the gravel before stopping right in front of me.

The headlights shone into my eyes and I looked away as I heard the whir of a window rolling down.

"Meggie?"

"Joe?" I said, surprised. "You're driving your dad's truck."

"Yeah. He's working, so I figured it'd be nice not to have to bum rides everywhere. What are you doing? I swear I saw you out here when I drove by before."

"Did you just say 'here' with a Southern accent?"

"What?" He got out of the truck. He was wearing jeans, dark blue and new-looking except for grass stains on the knees, and a gray T-shirt. One of his sneakers was untied. He was so good-looking it seemed like words needed to be invented to describe him. Something like gorgeosity. Or hotiful.

"Here," I said again.

"Here?"

"Yeah." He did have a bit of an accent, a kind of drawl over his vowels. So that's what six months in military school got you. I smiled, imaging that on a brochure. *We Change Everything—Even The Way You Talk!*

"Okay," he said. "You've been drinking, right?"

"No. Why would I . . . oh. Because your dad does, you think everyone—"

"Nice," he said, and got back in the truck, slamming the door. "Real nice."

"I'm sorry," I said. "I wasn't thinking. I was just—I was just talking."

And I was. Joe was affecting me in a very weird way. Before the crash he was JOE and I couldn't do anything around him except stare. I'd spent so much time having feelings I knew were stupid because he looked like he did and I looked like Bonezilla that actually talking to him was something I'd never been able to do more than think about. But now that all those feelings were gone, now that I looked at him and just saw a guy, it was like my brain didn't know what to do with itself. And since we didn't have any connection, since he'd never seen who I used to be, since we'd never really spoken, I was apparently able to talk. To say whatever came to mind without checking to make sure it was something I was supposed to say.

I was able to just be me—the me who I was now.

"Talking, right," Joe said. "You and everyone else. 'Oh, look, there goes Joe. Just got home—wonder how long it'll take him to end up like his dad?'"

"People don't say that."

He looked at me.

"Okay, maybe some of them do. But not everyone does. Like Tess down at the dealership—people like her, they're more into your face and stuff. I mean, when you first got back all Mom did at dinner was bitch about how Tess took two-hour lunch breaks to meet you until you . . . you know. Moved on."

"My face and stuff?" He rested his head against the steering wheel. "Crap, you are drunk. Get in and I'll drive you home."

"I don't want to go home."

"Yeah, well, life sucks that way sometimes."

There wasn't much I could say to that, so I got in the truck. We drove in silence till we got back into town.

"I hate this fucking place," he muttered as we began to drive by houses.

"So why did you come back?"

He glanced at me. "I was tired of getting up at four a.m. to pretend I was in the army and didn't want to do it for real after I graduated. Plus it's really hot in Alabama."

"Oh."

He tapped the steering wheel with one hand as we turned onto our street. "No one—no one ever even came to visit me when I was there. It was like when Beth died my parents just . . . they stopped, you know? Everything fell apart."

"So you came back to—what? Make sure they saw you?"

"No. Maybe." He blew out a breath. "We're here."

"I told you I didn't want to go home."

"Fine. Then you'll have to sit in my driveway and hope your parents don't see you."

"Fine."

"Okay," he said, and pulled into his driveway, parked the truck. I could hear frogs and crickets chirping in the yard as he opened his door and said, "See you around."

"Wait," I said, and he paused, half out of the truck. "How come you haven't asked me about the crash? You're about the only person in town who hasn't."

"It's not like everyone doesn't know the story already," he said, and slid back into the truck, pulling the door closed and looking over at me. "Besides, between the thing with the roof and then tonight with you standing out in the middle of nowhere . . . I don't know. You seem a little . . . different than you were before."

"I—I am," I said. "But most people don't see that. They look at me and they don't even see me. They just see this thing, you know?" I shook my head. "Never mind."

"They see what happened with the plane and not you."

I looked over at him, surprised. "Yeah."

"Before Beth . . . before she died, people looked at me and saw what happened to my dad, what he did at Reardon Logging. And then, afterwards, they just saw her, a girl who died because no one in her family could stop fucking up long enough to be there for her."

He was silent for a moment, and so was I.

"You aren't going to say that's not true," he finally said.

I shook my head, because he was right and I saw no reason to lie to him. No reason to pretend.

"It sucks," he said. "People here look at you and see all

kinds of stuff, not about you, but about your family, and all you want is for them to look at you and see true."

"See true?"

"See you. Who you really are."

I nodded. "I didn't—I didn't know you were like this."

"Like what?" he said, his voice suddenly sharp. "That I can think?"

"Well, yeah. I mean, no, not like that. I know you think. It's just you're so—I mean, you've seen yourself in a mirror. Guys like you—"

"Guys like me graduate from their shitty military school and have their grandmother box up their stuff and put it out on the lawn when they won't join the army. Guys like me come home and realize we're not wanted by our own family. Guys like me are lucky to get a job, especially considering what their old man did, but pity goes a long way and everyone likes to tell them that. Guys like me end up sitting in their driveway talking to someone who runs around at night climbing up onto roofs or standing by the side of the road."

"Does this whole pissed-off thing usually work for you with girls? Because I'm not getting it at all."

He laughed, a startled sound, and then grinned. "I—you're the first girl I've actually talked to in a long time. Usually it's . . . you know."

"Oh. Right. So when you stopped, were you—I mean, did I mess up plans you had or anything?"

He shook his head. "Nah. I was just visiting someone." He tapped his fingers against the steering wheel. "Did you mean what you said about how people see you?"

I nodded.

"So tonight and the other night . . . ?"

"I—I can't stand being Megan The Miracle. I'm not—it's not me. Do you know what I mean?"

He nodded and I looked out the windshield. My parents' bedroom light was on. I could see the curtains drawn back, see my father's face looking out at the road. I could feel his worry and my mother's calling me home, reminding me of what I was supposed to be. What I was.

I opened the truck door. "I gotta go. My parents are waiting up for me. Thanks for the ride."

He didn't say anything, but I thought I heard his truck door open and then close as I was walking down his driveway. I looked back when I reached the end, but the porch light had been turned off, and I couldn't see where he was.

Fifteen

I went to school even earlier than usual the next morning. I had to. Going downstairs and seeing David at the kitchen table reminded me why I'd left last night. I said I wasn't hungry, that I needed to get going.

David wouldn't look at me when I told him goodbye.

I went to the girls' locker room like I usually did and sat on the floor by the door. I stared up at the ceiling, counting the dots on each tile. My head felt heavy, and I leaned against the wall. I started counting dots out loud and then somehow I was in the kitchen at home.

Something had happened to the floor, and when I looked down I saw there wasn't a floor at all, just dirt. It was cool and dry against my feet. I wiggled my toes and wondered what had happened to my shoes.

"Megan," a voice said, and I looked up. Carl was waiting for me at the stove.

"I know you heard me," he said. "Why did you let go of my hand?"

I backed away, my feet sliding in the dirt and catching on hidden rocks. I could smell pine trees all around me. Carl came closer.

I didn't want him to. I didn't even want to see him. I tried to turn away but behind me everything was on fire, ground to sky glowing red-orange. I tried to scream, but couldn't because my mouth was full of water. I looked up and rain washed over me, the sky moving closer, the fire reaching for me, and Carl was right there, his hand—

I woke up then, a sudden, panicked jolt into alertness that left me shaking.

It was a dream.

I'd dreamed, I'd just fallen asleep, but what I'd seen had been so real that I could still feel the dirt against my feet. See Carl waiting for me. I took a deep breath and ran a hand over my face. It was wet with tears.

I left school then. I hadn't cried since I'd woken up in the hospital. I hadn't cried when I first got home and stood in the bathroom wondering if I was dead. I hadn't cried when I realized I wasn't a miracle at all. I hadn't cried when I realized my parents didn't want to see that something was wrong with me.

But now I was crying, and couldn't seem to stop. I could hear myself making noises, raw, hurt sounds, and I couldn't seem to stop them either.

I wiped my eyes as I got in my car and wished I could go somewhere that would make me whole again. But it wasn't going to happen because just driving was terrifying and painful; the trees made me tense, and seeing the hills off in the distance made me hunch over, holding the steering wheel so tight my hands ached.

I bit the inside of my mouth hard, using the pain to stop my tears, to quiet myself, and tried to focus. Why had I cried *now*? I'd seen Carl before, dreamed of him and fire and the forest. Maybe it was what he'd said about his hand, maybe I'd . . .

I couldn't think anymore—wouldn't—because I knew something really bad, like back in the gym or worse, was going to happen if I kept going. The church was up ahead, just around the corner, and I pulled into the office parking lot, shaking so hard my teeth were chattering.

I rested my head on the steering wheel and slid my shaking, sweaty hands under my knees, feeling them tremble hard and fast even though I was now sitting on them.

I felt like I was going to die, and I didn't want to.

Realizing that only made everything worse. All I could

think was that I could die, that I might die right here, right now, and my teeth started chattering harder, almost violently, my whole body shaking so hard it almost hurt. Something was wrong with me, so wrong, and I thought about my dream, Carl reaching for me as the fire moved closer . . .

"Megan." I looked up, startled, and saw Margaret peering at me through the driver's side window.

"I don't mind if you want to sit out here," she said, "but you'll need to be out of the parking lot by two because we're having it resurfaced." She paused for a second and then said, "Why don't you come inside and sit down? You seem a little upset and I can call your mother or father and have them come get you."

"No." That was the last thing I wanted, to have to be Miracle Megan right now. "I—can I just come in and sit down for a minute? I just . . . I need to . . . I need to not be in the car right now."

She nodded and so I got out of the car and went inside.

Margaret's office was small; it had a desk that held a computer and printer, two chairs, and a small bookcase filled with monthly Bible guides that the church sold. Some of them dated back to before my parents were born.

"Here," she said and pointed at the chair on the other side of her desk. "Sit."

I sat, and she left and came back with a glass of water. She gave it to me and then got out her purse and dug around in it for a while before handing me an old-fashioned peppermint candy, a red and white swirled circle wrapped in plastic. "Eat this. I thought I had a candy bar in here but the Gaines girl must have taken it last Sunday after the service. If her mother would stop telling her she needs to lose ten pounds, she'd probably stop running around taking candy out of people's purses when she's supposed to be setting up the covered dish supper."

"Emily Gaines?" Emily was a very pretty tenth grader who was almost as awfully thin as I used to be. If she lost ten pounds, she'd be nothing but Barbie hair and bones.

"Yep. Finish your water." She sat down at her desk and started typing. "No school today?"

I put the glass on the floor by my chair, looking down as I did. "I—I'm doing a special project. So I get to leave early."

"Nine in the morning is pretty early."

I shrugged. Her fingers flew over the keys. "You type really fast."

"That I do. You're practically born knowing how to type now, but when I grew up we all had to take typing and didn't pass unless we typed sixty words a minute. I got along fine till computers came along and then . . . well, you can guess what kind of adjustment that was."

I nodded, even though I couldn't. I couldn't even picture

not having computers, and the only time I'd seen a typewriter was in an old movie I had to watch for school in seventh grade.

When Margaret was done, she printed out a couple of pages and got up, motioned for me to follow her. "You can help me make the bulletin for next week's service."

We photocopied pages on a tiny copier that jammed a lot and then folded the bulletins. It took forever because Margaret said I didn't line the edges up right. When we were done we took them over to the church and put them on a table in the hallway just inside the front door, and then Margaret said she'd make me lunch.

I said, "Okay."

When we got to her house, she made me drink another glass of milk. I got up to look at the plants in her living room and dumped half of it on them while she made peanut butter sandwiches. Next to the plants was a picture of Rose, smiling and holding a bingo card. I wondered if Margaret missed her, then thought of the bedroom I'd seen and how it held so much of Rose, and knew she did.

"You did tell your parents you were here the other day," she said after I finished eating my sandwich.

I nodded. She squinted at me and then slid her glasses back up her nose. "Good. I hope you don't want dessert, because all I have is applesauce."

I shook my head. "Look, about the other day, I don't want you to think that I think you and Rose were—well, you know how some people in town are. But they're totally wrong. Rose was great. Not that you're not nice too. It's just that I never thought—I mean, I know that plenty of people are . . . you know. But I just didn't think about it in Reardon."

Margaret raised both eyebrows. "How eloquent. But I think I understand what you're saying, and yes, Rose and I didn't go out of our way to talk about our life together. I love Reardon, but it's a small town and people here, especially back when we first bought the house—they had very definite thoughts about things, and we just weren't up to trying to change that. We'd spent enough time trying—and failing—to make people see what was really going on in Vietnam after we got back from the war. And I also had my parents to think about. They were very old-fashioned, but I loved them dearly."

She got up and went into the living room, came back with a photo that she handed to me.

I looked at it. It was of a much younger Margaret and Rose, standing in front of their house. Margaret had one arm around two older people who had to be her parents, beaming and holding a SOLD! sign, and Rose was staring at the camera, her hands clenched tight by her sides.

"My parents died about a year after this was taken," Margaret said as I gave the photo back to her. "I hadn't expected to lose them so soon." She touched both their faces, and then rested a finger under Rose's unsmiling face.

"I was so worried about Rose back then. She had a rough time our first year here. Lots of nightmares she wouldn't talk about. She felt bad too, like she wasn't herself, she'd say. Like she wasn't real. And I knew there were things she couldn't remember about the war, that she—that I think she wouldn't let herself remember. But whenever I'd ask, she'd pretend everything was fine."

"What happened?"

Margaret put the photo down and looked at me for a long moment, like she was considering something. "She got through it as best she could. She remembered some things and made her peace with what she couldn't or wouldn't. It was always with her, of course, but the parts of her that were so hurt got better. The mind—" Margaret tapped her head with her fingers. "It's very resilient." She looked at the photo again and then said, "Do you talk to your parents about the crash?"

"I—no."

"Why not?"

"I don't know."

"Well, you should."

"I don't—I don't need to," I said through gritted teeth.

"Believe me, I know what they think. What a miracle I am."

"I think you're underestimating your parents," Margaret said, but she was wrong.

When I got home, Mom was there, in the kitchen, defrosting chicken.

"The school called," she said, "so I came home early to see how you're doing." The microwave beeped and she opened the door, poked the chicken with a shaking hand, and then restarted it. "You're feeling all right, aren't you?"

I knew why the school had called. I hadn't shown up for any classes. They had to call.

"I'm fine," I told her, and waited to see what she'd say.

"Of course you are," she said—*of course, of course*—and smiled at me. "Do you want something to eat?"

"Sure," I said and ate chocolate chip cookies while Mom finished defrosting the chicken and then put it in the oven. She didn't ask me anything else, and her hands never stopped shaking. I ate cookie after cookie but I still felt hollow inside, and when I went upstairs and lay down I knew I didn't want to close my eyes.

Sixteen

After that phone call, things started to change at school.

My teachers started asking me to pay attention. They started asking me why I hadn't done my homework. They asked me to please stop looking around and focus.

I didn't pay attention. I didn't do my homework. And I kept looking at the empty seats in my classes, and Carl or Sandra or Henry or Walter would be there. They could sit and wait for me forever. They had nowhere else to go. They'd never told me that, but then, they didn't have to. Just them being there was enough.

Too much.

The extra time I'd been given for tests disappeared. I started getting them back with red Fs scrawled across them, and the understanding nods I'd gotten when I presented my empty hands instead of homework were replaced with frowns and more scarlet Fs. My guidance counselor pursued me in the halls, pressing me to turn in part of my independent study and set a schedule for the rest. She suggested that I come by her office, told me that we needed to talk. She said she noticed I'd been absent a lot. She said some of my teachers were concerned.

She didn't mention my parents.

After that phone call, things changed at school, but not at home. There everything was the same. Everything was *fine*, and on Sunday, I sat between my parents in church, squeezed in by their love, and wanted to scream.

I didn't, though. I just sat there, standing when I was supposed to, sitting when I was supposed to, a smile pasted on my mouth and my hands clamped into fists, nails digging into my palms. I saw Margaret looking at me, but pretended I didn't see her.

The next day, David said he didn't feel well. Mom made him go to school and that night, at dinner, he sneezed and coughed the whole time.

"I'm cold," he said as we were supposed to be eating our meatloaf, and sneezed twice in a row.

Dad looked at him when he said that, concern on his face. Mom did too, and watching David light up under their gazes made something inside me hurt.

"Why don't you excuse yourself and watch whatever you want on TV. If you're getting sick, I don't want Meggie to catch it," Mom said. Dad nodded and the two of them looked at me. Me, not him.

David stood up and pushed his empty chair into the table hard, making it rattle. No one said anything when he left the room.

I asked to be excused after that and went to the living room, stood in the doorway looking at David. He was lying on the sofa watching some cops arrest an old guy who was driving on a suspended license. I wanted to say something but David turned up the television as soon as he saw me.

"David," I said, and then paused because I didn't know what else to say. He looked at me, and then he turned the TV up more, coughing as he did. Mom and Dad still didn't come to check on him.

At home things were the same, but at school they kept changing.

My guidance counselor called Mom and Dad to talk about the work I wasn't doing and the deadlines I'd missed for my independent study. They never told me about the call. I only found out because of Coach Henson.

He came up to me in the hall as I was leaving school, as I pushed past Carl, who was standing in a corner tapping one fist against his chest.

"Meggie?"

I jumped when I heard Coach's voice, and when I looked over at him he was frowning, the lines on his forehead and between his eyes mirroring his mouth. I forced myself to smile, and knew it hadn't come out right.

"I need to talk to you," he said, glancing away from my bared teeth. "I was in guidance earlier, and they're calling your parents. Apparently they've talked to your mother before but . . . anyway, it sounds like you're having some problems with your grades and your independent study."

I shrugged.

The furrows on his forehead and between his eyes grew deeper. "Look, no one is saying you aren't capable, and I'm telling you about the calls because I believe in you. I know there have been big changes in your life and with change comes . . . well, change. But turning your back on your talents, your team, and not following through on assignments—that's not acceptable, not on any level. Do you understand what I'm saying?"

I wasn't sure he even understood what he was saying, but I could tell he meant well. Everyone did. Everyone wanted me to keep being a miracle.

"Thanks, Coach," I said, and went home.

Mom and Dad didn't talk to me about the phone calls. Instead, Mom came up to my room that night. I was sitting cross-legged on the bed, staring gritty-eyed out the window. Once in a while I checked the clock to see how much time had gone by. It was always less than I thought.

"I came to see how you are," she said, and put an arm around me. I looked at her fingers, felt them tremble on my arm.

"Fine," I said and felt her hand relax.

"Studying?"

I looked at the closed books on the floor by my desk, the notebook lying caught in the footboard at the end of the bed. Dust was starting to mark its edges.

"I thought we might talk," she continued, as if I'd answered her question. "You seem—you haven't been talking about school much. How is it?"

Was she really trying to talk to me? Was she finally going to say she knew something was wrong with me?

"It's—I don't know." I took a deep breath. "I don't feel like I used to. I feel . . . different."

"Of course you do. You haven't exactly had a regular summer, you know. So it's no wonder that things seem a little strange now."

"It's more than a little strange," I said, and looked at her. "I don't feel like I'm really here. I feel like part of me is . . . different."

"Part of you is different, Meggie. I believe that when a

miracle happens it changes that person, and a little piece of them belongs to . . ." She pointed up at my ceiling and then smiled at me.

I stared at her.

I stared at her, and I—I wanted to hit her. I wanted to hit her so badly I was shaking with it. "You think that how I feel is—you think I'm part God?"

"No, nothing like that." She reached for me and I drew back, pushing myself as far away as I could. Her smile trembled, but she kept talking. "You've been touched by Him and I just—I wanted you to know that your father and I love you and that we know how special you are. Maybe other people don't see how much, or don't understand what you've been through, but we do. We know—"

"I get it," I said, my voice fast and loud, too loud. "You know what I am."

I was afraid to move. I knew if I did I'd do something. That I'd hurt her. When she finally left, a kiss on my cheek and a whispered, "Good night," I uncurled my stiff body and lay there, wondering what would happen when I couldn't pretend to be what they needed. What it would take to make them see I wasn't a miracle at all.

Seventeen

When the house was silent and dark, I climbed out the window and went for a run.

I ended up in the same spot I had before, the empty space between town and the road that ran around it. I stood there for a while, moonlight shining over me, but even though it looked just like it had the other night, it wasn't the same.

I didn't pass any trucks on my way home. I didn't see anyone.

When I got back to my street there was a truck at the far end, at the beginning of the road. It was pulled over to the side, its lights and engine off, and I realized it was Mr. Reynolds's. Joe was sitting inside. He didn't seem to see me and I watched him for a second, sitting there staring into the dark, and wondered what he was thinking about. He looked like he wanted to be alone. I could understand that.

I started walking back to my house. There were shadows on the side of the road, the trees, and they seemed to be reaching for me. I tried not to look at them.

"Hey," I heard, and turned around to see Joe leaning out his truck window. "How come you didn't say anything when you walked by?"

"You looked like you wanted to be alone."

"Oh. So it wasn't . . ."

"Wasn't what?"

"Nothing." He sounded upset.

"Okay. Bye." I didn't know what else to say. I turned away and started walking again.

I waited to hear the truck turn over and even moved a little toward the side of the road so he could drive by, but I didn't hear anything. I glanced over my shoulder and Joe was leaning out the window again. He still looked upset.

"Look," he said. "The other night you said all this stuff about everyone and we—you know, we talked, but now you don't even—you could have said something to me."

"You looked like you wanted to be alone."

"How would you know what I look like when I want to be alone? Up until you started jogging in the dark we've said maybe four words to each other."

"I—wait. You're mad I didn't say 'hi' to you when you were

sitting alone on the side of the road in the middle of the night?"

"It sounds stupid when you put it like that." He sounded embarrassed. "I just thought . . . oh, forget it."

We sort of stared at each other for a second. He looked away first, looked down at the road. In the moonlight, his black hair shone. Beth's hair had been almost the same color and I realized that's who he'd been thinking about, sitting in the truck in the dark.

I scuffed one sneaker along the road. "Did you—did you ever tell Beth about the time you tried to drive to Grant's?"

He looked at me, surprise on his face, and then he laughed. "You remember that?"

"Let's see, the police calling on a Saturday morning to say that the seven-year-old next door had driven into my dad's car? Yeah, I might remember that."

He got out of the truck, shaking his head, and hopped onto the hood. There were faint green stains on the knees of his jeans again. "You know I couldn't even reach the pedals of my mom's car? It only rolled down the driveway because she'd forgotten to put the parking brake on so when I started it . . ." He made a forward motion with one hand. "Man, did I get in a lot of trouble for that, and all because I wanted to go to Grant's and get that cereal with the marshmallows shaped like baseball bats. And then Grant's closed almost right after and for the longest time I thought it was because of what I did."

"Really?"

He shrugged. "Yeah. Do you remember when they closed?"

I nodded. "I didn't get why it was such a big deal that Mr. Grant died at first, you know? And then the store was gone and if we ran out of milk or something, we had to drive out of town to get it. Oh, and I've never seen those cups of ice cream with the little wooden paddles anywhere else. I used to look for them every time we went to the grocery store."

"I'd forgotten about those," Joe said. "I used to love them. Beth—" He looked down, rapped one hand softly against the truck hood. "I took her into Grant's after it was closed once. Her class was going on a field trip to Derrytown to see animals in a petting zoo or something, and she couldn't go because animals made her asthma real bad, so I told her I'd take her someplace."

He looked up and smiled at me. "She said she wanted to go somewhere no one else in town could go. So I pried open the back door and took her inside. Remember that picture of Mrs. Grant that was up front by the cash register? It was still there."

"Did you tell her the story about you and the cereal?" The wind picked up and the trees scraped, branches screeching. I tensed, pleating my fingers into the hem of my running shorts, twisting the fabric.

"Yeah. She thought it was funny. Of course, she thought it was funny because I didn't know you had to use the gas and brake pedals to drive. You know, you look like you're gonna fall down. Do you want to—?" He pointed at the truck hood. I looked at it, and then up at the trees hanging over it. None of them were close enough to touch it.

I walked over to the truck and sat on the hood. I leaned back a little as I did, bracing my hands behind me. It was easier to turn my head and keep an eye on the trees behind us that way. "Thanks."

He glanced at me, then looked back at the road. "I still can't believe you remember the car thing."

"My father, the insurance guy, having to file a claim for an accident caused by a seven-year-old? He still tells people—well, you know how it is. Everyone tells the same stories over and over and over again. There's like, what, ten of them for the whole town?"

He laughed. "Eleven."

"Well, it'll hit twelve about ten minutes after David turns sixteen and manages to talk my parents into getting his learner's permit. You've seen the damage he can do on a bike."

He didn't laugh at that, just rapped one hand against the truck hood again. "People are saying . . . I've heard some stuff about you at work."

"Yeah, I was in a plane crash. I know that."

"No, not that. Other stuff, like how you're never in school, and when you aren't there you're . . . um . . ."

I stared at him. "What? Hanging out with the town lesbian? Let me guess, you want details. I mean, guys like lesbians, right?"

"Meggie—" He reached out and put a hand on my arm. "I just meant that I've heard you're voluntarily hanging out with Margaret."

I pushed his hand off. Hard. "*Gay* Margaret. Right?"

"God, you sound like the guys at work. I said Margaret. You know, old and really crabby? Gives out boxes of raisins on Halloween and says things like, 'You look just like your grand-father. He was beautiful, but kind of soft in the head.'"

"Oh." I said. "Yeah. I . . . we've talked a few times. Well, she does most of the talking. Did she actually say that stuff about your grandfather?"

"Yeah."

"To you?"

He gave me a look.

"Okay, stupid question. But when did you two ever talk? I mean, you don't go to our church or anything."

"Back when Beth was—it was because of Beth. She really loved stuffed animals. Remember that?"

I nodded.

"She couldn't ever have a dog or anything like that, you know, so she had this whole zoo in her room instead. And Rose . . . Rose gave her a bunch of teddy bears one year, right after Christmas." He paused. "You went to church with her, so you know why she had the leftovers."

I nodded again.

"It sucked for Rose," he said quietly. "But it was nice for Beth. She loved those bears. And then—well, you know how Beth was. Rose told her she'd made them and Beth decided she wanted to learn how. So my mom called over there and once a week until Rose died, Beth would go over there and make bears with her. And whenever I had to pick her up Margaret would always tell me stories about my grandfather and how he was before he left town and my grandmother. And while she was doing that she'd make me—"

"Drink a glass of milk. She still does that. Doesn't care if you hate it either."

He laughed, leaning toward me, and his breath blew warm against my cheek. "You know the stuff I said earlier? I thought—I thought maybe you were blowing me off because of what I said the other night."

"Why would I do that?" Usually when someone was this close to me, I wanted to move away, but I felt okay with him.

I felt like he looked at me and saw me. The real me, and not a miracle.

"I don't know. I said some . . . stuff."

"So? I said some stuff too."

"So we both said stuff, huh?" He grinned at me, and even though the trees were swaying, leaning in close, for a second I only saw his smile.

Eighteen

Two days later, Jess spoke to me.

I had gotten to school late, my legs aching as I cut across the parking lot. I'd kept running at night, the same long looping track around town, and the muscles on the front of my thighs and on the back of my legs hurt constantly. Even my calves were sore.

It was cold out now. Fall had come the way it always did, dropping in overnight and sucking the last of summer dry. I had felt it showing up, the wind chilling my legs as I'd run last night, my breath misting as I'd climbed up to my room before reluctantly dropping inside.

When I walked into school, Jess was standing there, waiting. The bell for first period had already rung and we were the only two people in the hallway. She didn't look at me and I figured she was waiting for Brian. She was twirling her hair, and her curls caught on her promise ring, covering the tiny diamond.

"Hey," she said, tugging her fingers free, her voice shaking the way it always did when she was upset, and I knew then she'd been waiting for me.

"Hey. Lissa said . . . she told me about you and Brian. Congratulations."

She smiled at me, her face lighting up. "Thanks. We looked at rings and there was this one that's so beautiful. I told Lissa that when I tried it on I just knew—"

She paused, tilting her head a little to one side, curls falling over her forehead, and her smile faded, her eyes filling with tears. "You don't care, do you?"

"Jess . . ." I looked down at the floor, already scuffed with shoe prints even though the day had just started, and felt like that. Worn out. Down. "I know how much you love him, and . . ."

"And what?"

"And you'll be happy," I said. "You'll be really happy together. Look, I gotta go to the guidance office and talk about my independent study, so—" I looked at her. She was trying to look angry, but she'd always been terrible at it. She just looked hurt instead. "I'll see you in class, okay?"

"Can't you stay and talk for just a second? I've been so mad at you for blowing me off and making Lissa cry, and I'm still mad at you, but I think that if we talk then maybe . . ." She kept talking and I tried to listen. I really did, but her words slid right off me.

She made a noise, a strangled furious sob, and said, "I get that you don't care, okay, but Meggie, it's like you're not even here. Like now, when I was talking, you weren't even listening. You looked—" her voice cracked, and she took a step toward me. "What's going on with you? Why don't you want to talk to me anymore?"

"I—" I started, and then shrugged.

"That's it?" she said, her voice rising. "That's all you do anymore, you know that? You say one word, maybe two, and then you shrug and vanish. It's like you don't care about anything. Something is seriously wrong with you."

Trust Jess to get it right, to really see me and come right out and say what no one else would. Everyone looked at Jess and saw a quiet, sweet girl. Almost no one got that there was more to her, that she always saw things for how they were and not as everyone wanted them to be.

For the first time in ages, I smiled at her and meant it. I saw her, and really felt our friendship.

"You're right," I said, and I felt our friendship, knew it was gone. I'd ruined it, and knowing that hurt. It hurt a lot.

"Meggie?" she said, blinking like she was surprised, but I

turned away and walked back outside, back into the cold.

I drove home. Mr. Reynolds was sitting in the backyard when I got there, his breath frosting the air as he sipped a beer and stared at a picture of Beth. He'd come home the morning after Joe and I had talked by the side of the road, and he'd left as soon as Joe came home from work that night, carefully backing the truck down the driveway and driving off. He didn't come back until Joe had to leave for work in the morning.

He did that every day, went out at night, all night, and then sat in the backyard during the day, drinking and looking at that picture and never seeing Joe.

I never even saw them speak to each other.

I thought about that, their silence and Mr. Reynolds sitting by Beth's grave like everyone knew he did. Mr. Reynolds, sitting by Beth like he could somehow soak her in before he left town again.

For some reason, it made me think about my parents.

My parents, who had started to wait up for me every night, sitting in their bedroom until they heard me swing up onto the roof and drop into my room. I would hear them moving around as I lay down to wait for sleep that wouldn't come, see the light from their room flicker off.

They'd stopped asking me how I felt and whenever I caught them looking at me I saw a deep, sad fear in their eyes. They knew something wasn't right about me, and I knew that was why they'd stopped asking me how I was. Why the fear was there. It hurt but I would see them watching me and knew that if I told them what was true, if I told them how lost I really was, it would break their hearts, and I couldn't bring myself to do that. I'd seen how much they'd suffered when David was born and even after they'd been told he'd get better. After he did get better.

I wasn't so sure that I could.

And so that night, when I climbed out onto the roof to run, I looked over at the Reynolds house. Moonlight was reflecting off the windows and I paused, staring at Beth's. The curtains were pulled closed like she was in there fast asleep and dreaming.

If it hadn't been for one day—just one day—she might have been.

Beth had died on a Tuesday. She'd taken the bus home from school, unlocked her front door and waved at my mother, who was waiting for David to get off the bus, and gone inside. She'd had an asthma attack an hour later. Mr. Reynolds was out at the county unemployment office, Mrs. Reynolds was on her way back from visiting her mother in Derrytown, and Joe was in detention for falling asleep in first period.

Beth did everything she was supposed to. She did her breathing treatment, and when that didn't work, used her inhaler.

When that didn't work, she called 911 and then went downstairs and sat by the front door to wait for the rescue squad. She stayed on the phone with an operator the whole time.

She died before the rescue squad got there.

Joe got home just as they were taking her out of the house. Mr. Reynolds got there soon after, and the police had to take Joe away so Mr. Reynolds wouldn't hurt him. Crazy with grief, everyone said. That's what everyone said to explain how Joe's family imploded, how Beth's death flung them away from each other. Her death was a loss they simply couldn't overcome.

I wasn't home when Beth died. I was over at Jess's, talking about Brian with her and Lissa, and by the time I did get home, the Reynolds house was quiet and dark, just like it was now.

I looked away from Beth's window, shivering, and climbed down onto the porch. My shadow fell over the porch light, and when I looked at it brightness flooded my gaze for a moment, my vision swimming gold and then shifting to a hazy, flickering red.

"Hey," I heard, and turned, saw Joe standing at the bottom of our porch steps, hands shoved into the front pockets of his jeans. He looked tired.

It was a relief to turn away from that red glow, even though spots of it danced in the corners of my eyes. "What are you doing here?"

He shrugged. "I saw you come out the window. When it

took you a long time to come off the roof I thought—for a second I thought you'd fallen or something. So I came over to make sure you're okay. Are you okay?"

"Yeah. I was just thinking."

"Well, okay then." He grinned at me, and I wondered what he remembered when he thought about that day. Did he remember everything? Did it make it easier, or harder?

"Actually, I was thinking about when Beth died."

His grin faded. "Oh." He took a step back and gestured at the empty driveway, his dark house. "I should go. Have a good run."

"Okay." I watched him walk down the driveway. It didn't take long for him to be swallowed by the dark. I made it about halfway down the driveway myself and then stopped because behind me, I thought I heard the sounds of someone—Carl—cracking his knuckles.

I wasn't going to turn around and look. I wasn't.

"You aren't running?" Joe said from the darkness at the end of our driveway.

I shook my head and heard the sound again. Knuckles cracking one by one, and my vision tunneled but wouldn't fade. Wouldn't let me go.

I sat down so I wouldn't fall down, feeling the world tilt around me. My head throbbed, a strange sparking pressure not like a headache but worse, like something inside me was trying to break free. I pressed my hands to my forehead, trying to make it stop.

"What are you doing?" Joe said. He was crouched down next to me, staring as I moved my hands away from my head, and I blinked at how close he was. I hadn't heard him walk over to me. There were grass stains on the knees of his jeans yet again. I tried to focus on them.

"I'm sitting." My voice sounded thick, far away.

He looked at me for a second more and then glanced over at his house, lifting his gaze up to Beth's dark window.

"I still remember exactly what it looked like when I got home the day she . . . the day she died. There were all these cars, all these flashing lights, and our front door was open a little bit. I could see people inside, just standing there, and then . . . then I saw her feet. They were bare and that's when I knew. She wouldn't go anywhere unless she had her shoes on, was always afraid she'd step on something and have to go to the emergency clinic for a shot. She hated that place so much, hated getting shots . . ." His voice cracked, and he fell silent. He didn't stop looking at her window.

"The guy sitting next to me on the plane hated shots too," I said. "He had a heart attack and had to get one in the emergency room, medicine or something, and he said he told them to just go ahead and let him die because he didn't want any needles . . ." I trailed off, something lurching sickly inside me.

Carl had told me that story. He'd told me about his heart attack and the emergency room doctor who had given him the shot he didn't want and how he'd woken up to see his wife crying over him and saying he was lucky, so lucky.

I hadn't remembered that before. The memory had just come and suddenly I was there on the plane, watching Carl stretch out his hands to show me how big the needle was, exaggerating its size and then thumping his chest with a fist to show his heart was still beating. Smiling at me until I smiled back, then dipping one hand into his shirt pocket and pulling out a picture, saying, "This is Owen. Turns two tomorrow. Came back early to go to his party and steal me some of that birthday cake when Gladys isn't looking. Forty years we've been married, and that woman's eyes are still as sharp as when I first saw her."

Oh God. Carl had been coming to see his grandson, his family, to be with Gladys. He was going to go to a birthday party. He was going to eat cake. I remembered all of that, could hear his voice, his story, and instead of going home he'd—

Joe touched my arm. I flinched, pulling away, and stood up. "I—"

"Sorry," he said. "I didn't mean to—I know you were thinking about what you said. About that guy. But I just . . . I was thinking about it too. What it was like for them at the end, I mean. And I think it was . . . I think it was okay for them, that when—that when death comes, it doesn't hurt. I think you just slip away. So they didn't know, you know?" His voice was so quiet. So hopeful.

So wrong.

"Beth didn't just slip away," I said, and my voice was so fast and so angry it sounded like it belonged to someone else. "She knew she was dying and everyone on the plane knew because when you die like that, when there's time to feel it, you know. You can't not know because you feel how much it hurts, how much everything hurts, and you're afraid and alone and—"

"Shut up," he said, standing up too and taking a step back, away from me. "She wasn't—Beth didn't—everyone said she didn't feel a thing. Everyone—" He let out a noise, like a gasp but sharper, more raw. "What do you know anyway? You walked away from that crash and left everyone behind. You don't know what happened to them, how they—"

"Stop," I said, a weak whisper, and felt something inside me give way, stumbled and sank down onto my knees. What if—what if he was right? What if I'd seen someone who was alive and left them? Had I done that?

I lay down and all around me the grass turned from night

dark to burning red flame. I tried to move away but there was nowhere to go. The grass flickered, drawing closer, and I saw it wasn't grass at all. The ground was pure flame, melting metal and dirt, and my feet were bare, my hands holding melted rubber and flailing, circling the air like a kid flapping his arms when he pretends to fly.

I couldn't get the flames away. They were crawling closer and closer, coming for me, and I—

"Megan, what are you doing?" Joe was staring down at me, a strange look on his face. I was curled up into myself on the lawn, knees tucked into my chest. My arms were outstretched, shaking, and they stilled as I saw the darkness around me, felt the wet, cold grass soaking into the back of my shirt.

"I . . . the grass wasn't here, there was fire and I—" I clamped my mouth shut as the look on his face grew stranger still, then sharpened with understanding. I stood up, biting the inside of my cheek hard so I wouldn't sway, wouldn't break open now, and wiped bits of grass off, focusing on their slippery feel.

When I finally looked at him, he was looking at me, and I saw that his eyes were blue, a strange dark blue, beautiful. I'd always thought his eyes were brown. Over ten years of living next door to him, over ten years of my heart slamming into my chest whenever he was near, and I'd been so hung up on him that I'd never really seen him.

He had blue eyes, and there were tears in them.

"I'm sorry about before," I said. "What I said about Beth, I mean. I—I was upset."

"But you were right." He stared at me, eyes glistening, and I saw so much grief and understanding there that I had to look away. "She . . . she must have been so afraid. She was always so scared when she had an attack. It was the one thing she couldn't—she could never learn enough to stop them. She shouldn't have been alone. I—I told her that when I saw her, when it was too late and . . ." He sniffed once. "Fuck. I should have been there. I tell her that every time I see her."

I looked at him and thought about the grass stains on his jeans, how I'd seen them over and over again. "You—you go and see her just like—"

"Yeah. Just like my dad. The one thing we have in common, except I don't drink when I'm there. Not that we ever talk about it or anything. He won't even say her name."

He blew out a breath. "I have to move out, you know. Having me around when he's home makes it harder for him." He glanced over at me. "Guess you know that. Kind of hard not to hear, right?"

"Yeah. I—sorry."

Joe nodded. "Guess you know he's gone again too. And that he took the truck with him."

"I heard him leave." We all had, during dinner. It had been impossible not to. He'd yelled, "No one asked you to come back here!" before he'd backed his truck down the driveway so fast we'd heard the tires squeal, slipping as he turned onto the road.

"He—I wanna hate him, you know? For being so . . . for being how he is. But I can't because everything—everything inside him died when she did but he . . . he's still here."

The front porch light flicked off and then on, and I looked over at the house and saw the shadow of my father through one of the tall, thin frosted-glass windows on either side of the front door.

"Oh. Guess my dad's up."

He glanced at the door, then back at me. "Do you think he knows I'm out here?"

"Don't know."

He nodded and then leaned over and gave me a hug, quick and awkward, like he wasn't used to giving them. Our front porch light flicked off and on again.

"He definitely knows I'm here," he said, and then turned around, headed back down the driveway, into the dark. I heard his feet crunch across the gravel scattered on the road, and then he stopped.

"See you around?" he said, his voice quiet.

"Yeah," I said, and turned toward the house. I heard Joe walking up his driveway as I went inside.

Dad was waiting in the front hallway. There was a sleep crease on his left cheek, and he was running one hand through his hair the way he used to when I'd sneak downstairs at night to see him and Mom talking about David back when they'd just brought him home from the hospital.

"Out kind of late," he said. "Especially on a school night."

I shrugged, and we both looked at each other. He was the first one to look away.

"You—you look tired, Meggie." He had his eyes closed, like he was hoping. Praying.

"I am," I said, and went to bed.

Nineteen

Coach Henson was in the parking lot when I got to school the next morning, and this time he pointed at me as I drove by, crooking a finger to show we needed to talk.

I pretended I didn't see him, and parked as far away from him as I could.

He came over right as I got out of the car, his face red from running or anger. Or both. "Guess you didn't see me."

I didn't want to deal with him and leaned against the car, pretending I was looking through the window for something inside. Maybe he'd take my silence for the hint it was and go away.

"Meggie, I'm talking to you."

Guess not. I looked at him, still leaning against the car. I was so tired I felt like I needed something to help hold me up.

"Sorry, it's just a little early for me. Not totally awake yet, you know?"

"I'm going to cut right to it," he said. "You still haven't checked in with the guidance office about your independent study project and your grades—well, if you were still playing soccer, you wouldn't be for much longer. At this point your parents are going to get a call and have to come in right away and talk about whether or not you're even going to graduate. What do you think about that?" He gave me a look, arms folded across his chest, clearly waiting for me to speak.

What could I say? *I want to care, but I don't. I look at you and all I feel is tired. I walk through school and all I want to do is leave. I wake up in the morning and don't know why I'm here. I feel like I'm not real. I feel like I died when everyone else on the plane did and I'm the only one who's noticed.*

I shrugged.

He threw his hands up in disgust. "That's it? That's all you've got? A shrug? I can't understand what you're thinking. Do you just not care or do you just not get it? I've bent over backwards for you. Everyone here has bent over backwards for you. And in return you've—"

"Let everyone down."

"So you do get it. Then the real question is, what are you going to do about it?"

"Nothing," I said, and got back in the car. He stood behind it, frowning, but when I started to back up he moved, shaking his head sadly.

I saw Jess and Lissa in Jess's car as I drove off. They were heading toward school, and pretended not to see me. I saw David too. His bus was pulling into his school and he was sitting in the back, knees up against the seat in front of him as he talked to his mutant friends. One of them saw me and waved, said something to David.

David didn't look at me. He just pressed his middle finger, pointing sky high, against the glass.

After that I drove around and ended up where I always did, in the empty area between town and the road that ran around it. I pulled the car over, parked in the empty space and turned it off, letting the silence of where I was sink into me. I could see the trees so clearly here, a dense tangle of green and brown that blanketed the hills, the ground rising higher and higher, up into the sky.

At night, I couldn't see any of this.

I tapped my fingers against the steering wheel and looked around my car. Aside from me, nothing in it was mine. Nothing was personal. No music, no food wrappers. Nothing. I didn't even have any school books around, left them all at home to gather dust.

I had always been a messy car person. I dropped papers on the floor of Mom's and spilled soda in Dad's. I lost socks I took off after games and forgot half-eaten candy bars until they melted or grew fur. In Lissa's car I had left notebooks and pencils and lost at least two calculators. In Jess's I had an extra pair of soccer cleats, and the sweater I'd worn the one time she and Brian and Matt and I had double-dated last year, which had been a disaster because Matt had talked about college soccer so much he'd bored even me. A week later, I'd won Athlete of the Year instead of him at the annual sports banquet and he'd dumped me.

I remembered having Mom and Dad drop me off at Jess's after the banquet, desperate to talk to her because I wasn't upset about Matt. I hadn't even cried.

"What's wrong with me?" I said to Jess. "I finally get a boyfriend—and it's not like there's a lot of choice around here—and I was glad when he said we were over. Glad! No more listening to him talking about trying to choose between Central State and Cedar College and that's not normal, is it? I should be crying, right?"

"It's totally normal," Jess said. "Matt so isn't the right guy for you. I mean, just because he loves soccer and you love soccer, it doesn't mean you're perfect for each other, you know? Now, tell me everything Coach Henson said after he called your name. Did he mention your six-goal game?"

I ended up spending the night, calling home and getting permission from Dad, who was completely distracted, more interested in talking to Mom about how David sounded like he was getting sick than in talking to me. Jess and I stayed up so late talking that her dad banged on the wall and told us that if we wanted to keep talking we had to go outside and do it in her car.

We had. Laughing, we'd trailed blankets out of her house and piled them around us in the car. We'd talked until the sun rose, falling asleep only long enough to wake up cold and stiff and exhausted. We didn't care, just got ready and drove to school with the windows down, the smell of the forest rolling in from the hills, the wind snapping across our faces and waking us up.

I'd been so happy. A happy that seemed so simple now— and so out of reach. I shifted in my seat, then slid over to the passenger side and closed my eyes. I pretended it was that morning again, that Jess and I were in the car, cracked the window and felt the wind stir across the top of my head.

Feel it, I told myself. Feel it. You're happy. You're in the car, it's early and the wind is blowing, catching your hair, and you're—

Cold.

I'm cold, shivering, and there is a woman standing in front of me. She is saying something. I can see her mouth move. There is sweat on her forehead, fat moist drops. I am so thirsty, and there is water dripping over my face but I can't seem to drink it. I can't seem to lift my arms to wipe it away.

The woman takes my arm and her hand is hot on my skin, burning me. I yank myself free, still shivering.

Honey, she says. Honey, where did you come from? I just came round the corner and almost hit you. Where did you come from?

I want her to shut up. Her voice hurts my ears. I point back behind me. I will not look.

I don't understand, she says.

There, I say. I was there. My voice hurts. I hurt.

The woman starts talking again and she is so loud. I put my hands over my ears. I can still hear her anyway, hear her saying, Were you in an accident? Did something happen to you? Did someone do this to you?

Honey, what's your name?

I don't know. I don't know who I am. I don't know who she is. I back away and she follows. She makes me take my hands off my ears.

Don't be scared, she says. My car is right here. See my car? You're safe now, honey. You're safe. I'm Joyce and you're safe. There you go, have a seat. I'm going to buckle your seat belt for you now, okay? There we go.

There is a window. There are trees all around me, so close, and

I am so tired and so cold that I'm falling. I am moving side to side, trapped in a seat with my vision narrowing down to black and yellow spots, and it's so warm behind me—so warm—and I know that if I turn around I'll see . . .

I have to get away. I try to move but I can't. I'm trapped. I can't get free. I can't—

I started to cry, shaking as a wounded noise ripped up my throat. It wouldn't come out, lay trapped inside me, and I couldn't breathe, felt the sides of my throat caving in. I buried my face in my hands, curling myself into a ball and willing my mind to go blank. I gulped in air, my heart knocking against my chest so hard I could feel it.

I had remembered something, finally, and I wished I hadn't.

Twenty

I cried so hard I ended up shaking uncontrollably, my chest hitching, and when I breathed I felt the weird spasm that snags your throat before you throw up. I couldn't seem to stop it.

I cupped my hands around my ears and dug my fingers in hard, scraping the skin beneath them. It hurt and I did it over and over again until my eyes watered and my head cleared, and then I crawled back into the driver's seat.

I didn't want to drive home—I didn't want to drive at all—but I couldn't stay where I was. Not with . . . I thought about what I remembered, what had happened to me, and shook my head, hard, as another sob shook me. In front of me, the trees shimmied, shaking in the wind.

I started the car.

I knew I was driving, that I was on the road, but I didn't

feel like I was. I felt like I couldn't reach the pedals even though I knew my feet were on them and the steering wheel felt like a puff of smoke, imagination in my hands.

I started counting out loud, hoping it would pull me back into myself. It didn't really work but I kept going because I didn't know what else to do. I was afraid to keep driving but was even more afraid to stop. What would happen to me if I did?

At 486 or 846—I couldn't remember what number I was on—I saw Margaret. I was at a stop sign, brake mashed to the floor so hard my foot hurt. She glanced at me and shoved her glasses up her nose, but didn't wave or anything. She wasn't walking like she usually did, like she was in a hurry and might knock you down if you got in her way.

Instead she was walking slowly, like she was in pain.

I rolled down my window. "Margaret? Are you . . . are you okay?"

"I'm fine," she said, and waved a hand at me, dismissal. "I know you must have seen people out walking before. Probably done it yourself when you aren't gawking at stop signs."

I wondered where she'd been walking and then remembered the church cemetery was out here, in a space we shared with another church in town. My mom sat on the board that hired someone to mow once a month and argued over how tall grave markers should be.

Margaret had been to Rose's grave.

When Rose died there had been a service at the church, but afterward only Reverend Williams, Margaret, and Rose's brother from Ohio had gone on to the grave. Rose hadn't wanted anyone else there when she was buried. The rest of us gathered in the church basement for a covered dish supper and when Margaret and Reverend Williams came back from the cemetery, Margaret unveiled an industrial coffeemaker that had Rose's name engraved on the base.

Rose had always been in charge of making coffee for the suppers and it had been famously bad—burnt or watery, or once, tasting like soap because she'd forgotten to rinse the pot out. Everyone had clapped and laughed through their tears and Margaret had said, "This is how she wanted to be remembered."

I bet Margaret didn't think of coffee when she thought of Rose, and I said, "Do you—do you want a ride home?"

Margaret straightened up, looked both ways, and then crossed over to my car, marched right up to my window.

"Listen up, Meggie," she said. "I'm not that old, and I'll have you know I'm still perfectly capable of going for a walk."

"I didn't say you were old. I just—"

"What are you doing out here anyway? And why are your eyes all red and swollen?"

"No reason," I muttered. "And I'm going, okay? I just thought maybe you'd want a ride home because you look . . . you look a little tired."

She snorted. "I do not look tired. And even if I was, I could get home just fine. I don't need you feeling sorry for me."

"I don't—"

"Oh, yes, you do," she said. "'Oh, look, there's Margaret, walking home from Rose's grave. Poor old Margaret—'"

"Fine," I snapped. "I do feel sorry for you. What's so horrible about that?"

She squinted at me, then stalked around to the passenger side and got in. When I didn't start driving right away, she sighed and made a 'go' motion with both hands.

We crossed over one street before she spoke.

"You're a fine one to talk about people feeling sorry for you, you know. People at church try to talk to you about what happened and you just stand there and nod until you think up an excuse to get your mother or father to take you home. Why do you do that?"

"I don't know."

She sighed, sharp and exasperated, but when she spoke again her voice was soft with understanding. "You don't remember everything about the crash, do you?"

I turned onto her street and stared blindly at the church,

seeing only trees and dirt and my bare feet. "I don't—I don't remember it at all."

She didn't say anything but when I pulled into her driveway she reached over and turned off the car. I sat there, staring at my hands clenched tight on the steering wheel.

She got out and said, "Meggie, come in and sit down for a bit, all right?"

She sounded just like always, the question more of an order, and her bossiness somehow made me feel better. Like at least someone knew what to do, and so I got out of the car.

Inside, I sat at the kitchen table while she did something over by the stove. After a while she put a glass of milk in front of me.

"Drink up," she said, pointing at the milk, and then sat down across from me.

I pushed the glass away and she sighed. "Your bones need calcium."

"I don't feel so good," I said. And I didn't. I felt hollowed out, which wasn't new, but around the edges of it, underneath, was something else. *Panic.* I could feel the memory of coming out of the forest after the plane crash pulling at me, dragging me down into a place of endless fear. Or remembering.

"I'm not surprised," she said. "Please drink the milk, Megan. There's sugar in it, and vanilla. It'll make you feel better."

I drank it. I never knew people put vanilla into milk. Why

would you even bother when there was chocolate around? But the smell of the vanilla made the milk taste softer somehow, and it did make me feel better. Calmer.

She got up and went into the living room while I was drinking and came back with an old paperback. The cover was gone and the pages were yellowed, curling up at the edges.

"I gave this to Rose a long time ago," she said. "A friend of mine from the war, a doctor, sent it to me after we moved here. It talks about the war and how it hurt people. We'd had dinner with him and his wife as we were driving out here and Rose . . . it wasn't a good night for her. She—well, she looked a lot like you do right now."

She tapped the book with one hand. "My friend was worried about her. I was worried about her. And you know what? She never read this book. She wouldn't even look at it."

She glanced down at it and sighed, and then she looked up at me. "For the first few months we lived here, I tried so hard to make Rose better and she hated it. She said she didn't want me trying to fix her. She said I made her feel broken and I—I finally decided that if I acted like everything was fine then eventually it would be."

She took a deep breath and folded her hands together. "But things weren't fine. Rose and I were happy but she—she was unhappy with herself for a long time. When I think back, I wish I'd told her to get help. I wish I'd said more, done more. But I didn't, and it wasn't until around the time your parents were first married that she truly felt like a real person again. Your mother probably remembers how Rose was before she was able to really face what had happened to her. You should ask her about it sometime."

"Why are you telling me this? What are you trying to say?"

"I think you know, Meggie," she said, looking at me until I looked away, "but I'll say it anyway. You need help, and you should start by telling your parents what you've told me."

"Yeah, sure," I said, and pushed away from the table, standing up. "I'll go do that right now."

"I don't think this will make you feel better, but you remind me so much of myself when I was your age," Margaret said as she stood up and headed toward the front door, opening it for me. When she looked back and saw my face, she laughed. "Now you definitely remind me of how I was at your age. Do yourself a favor and go straight home, Meggie. Talk to your parents. Really talk to them."

"It won't work," I said. "It won't help them at all."

"Oh, Megan," Margaret said. "Don't you get it? It will help *you*."

Twenty-One

When I got home, Mom was catching up on TV, sitting on the sofa in the living room fast-forwarding through the commercials with a pile of partially folded laundry beside her.

"Hey Mom," I said, and she looked up and gave me a huge smile.

"Some day off, right?" she said, and patted the space next to her. "Come sit with me."

I did, and she went back to folding socks. David's feet were already so big his socks were larger than Dad's. When the ads stopped she watched a little bit of TV and then stopped it, turning the television off and looking at me. I stared at the socks.

"So, you're home early."

From the way she said it, with a weird catch in her voice, I knew she'd already gotten the call Coach had told me about.

I glanced at her, and the look on her face . . . she looked like David used to when he was really little and first started trying to lift his head up. He was so sick that he couldn't do it. He'd wanted to do it—you could see it—but he couldn't, and Mom looked like that. Like there was something she wanted to say but couldn't.

Or wouldn't.

"Mom," I said, and when she looked at me my voice dried up. She looked so scared.

It was worse than the smiles, than the too-eager eyes. It was one thing to see my parents pretend. It was another to see that they knew something was wrong and had no idea how to fix it.

That they knew I was broken.

So we pretended, just like we had since I'd opened my eyes in the hospital room. I sat there, scared and lost, and faked a smile while she turned the TV back on and filled me in on what was going on so there was no room for me to say another word.

"Your father's coming home for lunch," she said when she got up to put the laundry away. I was digging my nails into my palms, trying to stay calm, to look normal. She was balancing the laundry basket on one hip, grasping it with her right hand while her left fidgeted with the television remote.

"There's his car now. Hear it?" She didn't wait for me to answer. "He and I have to go out for a little while this afternoon.

How does bologna sound? Or would you rather have grilled cheese?"

"Cheese," I said. Mom left, and I scrunched my knees up tight into my chest, trying not to hear them talking in the kitchen. I heard the words "school" and "meeting" and my mother sniffed like she was trying not to cry. I had to lie down but it wasn't like before, wasn't like when I was being pulled back into memories I now knew I didn't ever want to have.

I felt sick with anticipation, with something that felt like hope because I knew something was going to happen now. It had to. They couldn't avoid this—me—now.

But they did.

We ate lunch, or at least they did and I tore my sandwich into smaller and smaller pieces while Dad told us about his morning and then Mom told him about someone at the dealership who needed homeowners insurance. Dad wrote down the info and said he'd give them a call. They were both really happy to get me more soda or another half a sandwich, but were just fine with me not wanting anything too. They didn't say one thing about school but as they were finishing their food, Mom looked at the clock and said, "Well, George, we'd better get going."

That was it. That was all they said. They knew I was failing all my classes. They knew I wasn't working on my independent study. They knew I had missed a lot of school. They knew I hadn't gone today.

They knew I wasn't a miracle. They just didn't say it. Wouldn't say it.

I didn't say it either. I just fiddled with my glass of soda and said, "I guess I'll do some homework. Maybe get out the soccer ball and practice a little."

Mom and Dad said that sounded great. I was lying and they knew it. They were lying and I knew it. But no one said that.

No one said anything real.

I stayed in the kitchen after they left. Why bother going up to my room? I would be there soon enough, tonight, lying awake waiting for another day to begin. I'd go to school, if I could, and then come right back home and do it all again and again and again. That was how things were. How they were going to be.

My feet were cold. I could feel the floor, slick linoleum rubbing against my toes. I looked down.

I had socks on. They were thick wool socks, padded along the bottom. I used to save them for end-of-season soccer games, when the ground froze and the cold would soak up through my cleats. They'd always kept my feet nice and warm before. Too warm even, sometimes.

There was a cake on the counter, but I didn't feel like eating any of it even though I desperately needed the distraction. Food would do it now, but I wanted something different. I went over to the fridge. Inside was milk, soda, rolls, cheese, apples, and a package of hamburger.

My feet were still cold. I wiggled my toes, felt them press against my socks.

I picked up the meat. I'd make myself a burger. The kitchen would get warm when I cooked it, plus it would give me something to do. Something to think about. I dropped the package on the counter, pulled open the plastic that covered it. I pushed my hands into the meat.

As soon as I did, I was on the plane.

I can't find anything to eat in my bag. I was sure I had something saved for this part of the trip, but I guess I didn't. I wish I'd thought to get some actual food while I was stuck waiting in Chicago. Henry says something over the tinny intercom. It's raining so hard I can't make out the words. It doesn't matter anyway. I can already tell we're starting to descend because the trees are closer, and if he's telling us there's turbulence, well, the plane's been bouncing around ever since we took off.

I glance over at the people across the aisle as I shove my bag back under my seat. The park guy, Walter, has finally stopped fiddling with his hat and actually put it on. The annoying blond lady, Sandra, says she wishes she could call home and check on her baby. I wish she could too so she'd stop talking about it.

Carl cracks his knuckles for the four millionth time and says, "I
sure am hungry."

I sigh. It was nice of Carl to let me have the window seat, but
the knuckle cracking is driving me crazy, and I'm tired of hearing
him talk about his family. And his heart attack. And his wife and
how she won't let him eat cake. I reach down and check the pocket on
the side of my bag.

Food! Well, what the flight attendant on the way to Chicago
handed out after an old lady complained. I knew I had something,
but still, finding it there was like a surprise. That flight seemed like
forever ago.

I rip open the tiny bag of pretzels with my teeth and stare out
the rain-wet window at the clouds, which are gathering thick and
dark. I saved the pretzels till now because the last part of the flight
is so boring. Once you cross into Clark County it's all trees. The only
reason Reardon even has an airport is because of the Park Service.
Stupid forest. I remember how, on the flight out, when we took off
the trees seemed so close to the plane, kind of like they are now, so
close, so close, too close and—

And everything after is a blur of noise and heat and pain.

When I can think again, I'm hanging upside down, legs dangling
up into a smoky wet sky and this is what I think: My head hurts. I
had a bag of pretzels. Where are they? I smell smoke.

I smell smoke and dirt and there's rain on my face, in my eyes. It feels cool on my legs. Lying like this is giving me a headache, but I can't think of how to fix it. All I can think about are those pretzels. I don't know what happened to them.

I hear something. The thing is, it's not a sound. It's stillness. A strange, too-quiet stillness, like all the air around me has frozen.

Then the world explodes.

There's a rush of heat, so hot I feel it like a sudden sunburn on my skin, and then I see it, a huge ball of flame shooting up toward the sky and spreading out, dropping all around me. Part of it falls and I feel it land on my feet, see bits of it spark down toward my head. I think I should move, but all I can do is stare at the fire. It's so strange. Fire isn't heavy. It's light.

But this fire is heavy, and it's caught on my feet, rain pounding on it and making it flicker. It doesn't vanish, though, just sputters and flares up again. How does it do that? I close my eyes and try to figure it out, but it's hard because my head still hurts and there's rain everywhere and my feet are hot. I open my eyes and look at them.

My shoes are on fire, melting.

I can move then. I start shaking my feet, trying to get the flames off but they won't move and I can't turn, can't do anything but kick my feet at the sky.

Then I remember the plane.

I remember being on it. I remember opening my pack of pretzels and looking out the window. I remember seeing trees all around us, so close.

I'm in my seat. Upside down, rain and fire all around me, and I'm still in my seat.

The plane crashed.

The heavy fire on my shoes is a piece of the plane, covered with something, fuel maybe, hot and angry enough to burn even in the rain.

My shoes are still on fire. My feet are starting to hurt.

I jerk my arms down, fumbling for my seat belt. I find it, but it won't pull free. I yank again, my feet kicking at nothing, and it opens. I fall and hit something solid, slamming into it. It hurts, pushing all the breath out of me, but I am too busy trying to get my shoes off to notice.

I end up shoving my fingers into the back of them and pushing. Hot rubber melts against my fingers, my feet sliding free, and I wave my hands in the air, arms stretched out like I'm flying. The wind blows again, hard, and water pours into my nose and mouth and pushes my soccer cleats—my lucky shoes—off my hands.

I wipe the rain off my face and stare at my pink feet for a moment. They look so strange, so bright and wet and resting on ground that doesn't look like ground at all.

I touch it. It's metal. I'm still inside the plane. I look around. Where I am it almost looks like a plane still, except everything up is *down and there's a hole where the bottom of the plane was, showing a strange dark red-gray sky.*

There's another hole farther up, a long jagged one dotted with broken glass, and I can see where part of the outside of the plane has bent inside. The rest of the plane should be there. It isn't. Just the outside, more gray-red sky and fire and rain. I see a piece of foil caught on the edge of the hole, curling up into itself in the wind. There is a pretzel hovering above it, spinning in place before it is shoved away by the rain.

That's where my pretzels are. I was sitting down there. How did I end up here, still strapped in my seat?

I don't know.

Where's the seat next to mine? It isn't here. I wipe rain out of my eyes again and look at the hole where the plane was torn in two. Up by where my pretzels were. The seat is there. I can see it now. There's a pair of boots near it. They aren't mine.

That's all I can think. They aren't mine. They aren't mine.

I shake my head. It hurts.

I have to move. To . . . something.

Speak. Okay, yes.

Speak.

"Hello?" I say, creeping forward, my feet tender and slippery. It takes me a while to reach the seat.

"Hello?" I say again and when I do, a hand stretches out blindly,

knuckles raw red even in the rain. I scramble back, terrified, and end up almost falling out of the hole, my shorts catching on the jagged metal, rain smashing into my face as smoke fills my mouth and nose.

The hand is still reaching out.

It's Carl. Carl, who was sitting next to me. His seat didn't move. If the plane was turned right side up, if the holes in it could be pretended away, he would be ready to fly.

I move toward him. He is upside down like I was, blood dripping from his mouth. His eyes are open wide and sightless.

"Carl?"

He doesn't blink. He doesn't seem to see me.

I do not want to touch his hand. I touch his face instead, avoiding his mouth. His skin is warm. There is a pulse beating in his neck. I don't know if it's fast or slow. I can't feel it very well. I press harder, trying to check. He blinks but his eyes stay so empty and when he breathes it's so loud and so slow.

"Help me," he says, his voice a faint wheeze, and I grab the dangling end of his seatbelt and follow it up, pulling it open. I'd do anything to stop him sounding like that. To stop him staring with those empty eyes.

He falls hard but I grab him, taking his hand in mine, and start pushing back toward the hole I almost fell out of, pushing toward the rain and the smoky gray sky. He holds on tight and his breathing is louder than the rain, a thick rattling gurgle.

Where our hands join, the rain washes pink rivers over my skin. I try not to look back, to keep moving forward, but there is so much pink and he is moving so slowly, his hand growing heavier and heavier in mine. When I finally pull us free of the hole we fall into mud, rocks scratching my skin, and the rain is everywhere.

His hand falls away from mine and when I look back at him it's still clamped into the shape it was when it held mine. His eyes are still wide open, and the rain washes into them, over the bright red stain that smears his mouth.

"We made it," I tell him, "we're all right," but he doesn't blink, doesn't move and when I go back to him there is nothing to feel in his throat and his skin is wet and cooling. The rain smells like metal, like blood, and keeps pouring into his open eyes, making tears. I lean over his face, covering him from the rain, watching his eyes as I wipe his mouth with my shirt. He doesn't blink. His chest doesn't rise and fall. He doesn't see that we have lived.

"Come on," I say, pleading, but he doesn't answer.

Someone else does, though.

Someone else screams.

I look around, but there's nothing to see but rocks and metal and trees, hovering over everything at the edge of the smoky sky. There's another scream, louder this time, and I realize some of the rocks are actually part of the plane, that it's smashed into the ground and is on fire, disappearing.

I run over to it but I can't reach it. It's too hot, so hot the bottoms of my feet hurt, and I don't hear anything now except the rain.

Then I see Sandra.

She is trapped under the burning piece of plane and is trying to crawl out from underneath it. Her mouth is open, but she's been pushed down into the ground, mud all around her while the plane melts above her. I can see her hair, wet bright yellow, and her hands are clawing at the ground. I can't move. I want to, but I can't. All I can do is see her face, mud and fire swallowing her, her terrified eyes.

Her wedding ring shines yellow in the rain too, reflecting fire, and as it crawls up her she screams and screams and her body writhes like a snake, her skin—

"No!" I say, but the fire doesn't hear me. It keeps burning, and rain blows into my eyes and smoke pours up my nose and into my mouth, metallic and meaty. I gag, falling onto my knees. The ground is wet underneath me, and I stare at it, mud and pine needles oozing around me. All I see are Carl's eyes, so empty, and Sandra's eyes, so afraid. I see his stiff empty hand and her desperate clawing ones, and I don't want to see them. I don't want to see anything.

I have to find someone who can help. Henry. It's his plane. He will know what to do. He will be able to make things better. I will find Henry.

I can't. I can't find him. I can't even find the cockpit. I find a piece of it, twisted metal holding broken gauges, but Henry is gone, and so is the door that he closed before we took off. It's like he wasn't even on the plane.

I do not want to find Henry anymore. I don't want to see what's left of him.

What do I do now? I don't want to look around anymore, but I don't know what else to do. I am wet and the fire is still burning, flames all around me. I don't know how to get through them. I wish there was someone here. My feet hurt. Why is there a hat on the ground?

Walter. It's Walter's hat. Where is he? Why do I see his hat but not him? Maybe he lost it like I lost my pretzels. Maybe he's wandering around just like me.

"Walter?" I call. The rain washes my voice away.

I say his name again. He doesn't reply, but there is something closer to the trees, another piece of plane that isn't burning. It isn't a big piece, but it's large enough to cover someone, and it's just lying there, wet in the rain. I walk toward it calling, "Walter?"

He doesn't answer, but he's there. I can see the top of his head. I push at the metal. It doesn't move. I push harder, and it scrapes slowly across rock, shows a slight dip between two large stones.

Walter is there. He is resting inside the stones. He isn't wet at all. He looks fine. His eyes are closed, but there is no blood, and I know he just needs to wake up like I did. I touch his shoulder.

Then I see his legs.

They aren't legs anymore. They are—they are ground up, split open, wedged broken into the rocks, his insides on the outside, and it looks like meat, he looks like meat, but his mouth isn't open, he isn't screaming, he just looks like he's asleep. I just imagined what I saw, I didn't see it and I will wake him up and everything will be all right.

"Walter, wake up," I say. He doesn't open his eyes. The wind blows, catching his hair and pulling it. It pushes rain over us, water washing down, soaking him, running down into his legs only they aren't legs at all anymore.

I fall down. I am not running but I fall anyway. I hit the ground hard and there is dirt in my mouth. The rain washes it away. I see Walter's hat. It is still lying on the ground. I should get up and get it but I don't want to move. I don't want to see anything else.

It is very warm behind me. I feel heat on my back, my legs, and my feet. The fire is spreading. I hear it too, popping and hissing.

Walter's hat blows away. The wind takes it up into the air, off into the trees.

I forgot about the trees. I saw them, but I forgot they were there. I look at them. They look angry. They are blowing in the wind, whipping around like they need to grab something, someone. I can't see Walter's hat anymore. The trees have eaten it. I shouldn't have looked at them.

My head feels strange, hot, and I reach up and touch it. My hair is on fire. The ends of it are burning, sizzling away.

I stare, and then I am running. I don't know how or where but I am. I am clumsy though, and I fall, landing hard on the ground. Rocks cut into me, rain tasting like dirt and metal on my lips splashing over me, and overhead the sky flares bright red and smoky. I think of Carl, lying on the ground and Sandra, clawing and struggling as her ring shone fire-bright. I think of Walter's hat and his legs.

Everything starts to dim, going dark, and I am glad. I don't want to see anymore.

When I woke up the sky was burning.

Twenty-Two

I was still in the kitchen when Mom and Dad came back. I saw them through the window. They were sitting in Dad's car, and they both looked upset. Dad kissed Mom, and she wiped her eyes. They both looked at the house and saw me. Mom got out of the car. Dad waved at me and then backed down the driveway. I looked down at the counter. At my hands. I went over to the sink and started washing them.

I couldn't stop thinking about what I'd seen. What I'd remembered. I was still washing my hands when Mom came into the kitchen.

"Are you cooking something?" she said. "You should wait and wash your hands after you're done with the hamburger."

I'd washed all the soap away but I kept rubbing my hands

together under the water. I could still feel meat on them. I could still see it.

"Meggie, you're going to rub your hands raw. And how long has this hamburger been sitting out? It looks—"

"I remembered the crash." My voice sounded fine. I was surprised by that. It should have sounded raw, broken. But it didn't.

"Remembered?" Mom's voice didn't sound fine. She leaned over and turned the faucet off. Her mouth was open, trembling. "Of course you remember it."

"I didn't. I woke up in the hospital and didn't know where I was or what had happened. You and Dad had to tell me."

"But then you remembered." When I didn't say anything she rested both hands on the counter, leaning against it. "You might have forgotten a few details but that's no reason to say—"

"Details?" I said, my voice rising, cracking. "I forgot seeing Carl die after he asked me to help him. I forgot watching Sandra burn to death. I forgot seeing what was left of Walter. Those aren't details."

She paled. "Meggie—"

"They aren't details," I said, shouting now. "They were people, they died, and I saw all of it and forgot. How could I do that? How could I forget what happened to them?"

"Megan, please don't—"

"What? Don't talk? Don't tell you that I was holding Carl's

hand when he died? Don't tell you that Sandra screamed until she couldn't anymore but kept looking at me, and that her eyes—"

"Don't do this to yourself. Don't blame yourself for living, for being a mir—"

"Stop! Stop pretending everything is fine. Stop pretending I'm fine." I leaned toward her, and she shrank back against the sink. "Tell me why I lived when they died and then tell me why I'm such a fucking miracle."

She started to cry. "You *are*," she said, reaching out to take my hands in hers.

"Liar," I said, and walked out of the room. Out of the house. She came after me, grabbing my arm as I reached the end of the driveway. She was still crying, her face red and wet, and she tried to pull me to her.

I pushed her hands away and her face crumpled, her expression going lost, frightened. "Megan, everything is fine. You're fine, sweetie, you really are. Just listen to me—"

"No," I said. And then I walked away.

The thing was, there was nowhere for me to go. All I had was town, bounded by the trees and hills, a border I didn't want to see, much less cross. I walked to the end of the road anyway and then started running, hoping my long strides would take me away from myself.

It didn't work. My mind stayed full of what I'd remembered

in the kitchen, everything I'd forgotten so *there* that now it was all I could see. I ran by Lissa's house, and then I ran by Jess's. They were both home but I knew I couldn't go and talk to them. I wouldn't know what to say. I headed toward the church instead.

Margaret was inside practicing on the organ. She took one look at me and stopped playing.

"You told them." It wasn't a question.

I nodded.

"You need water," she said, and pulled a bottle of it out of her enormous purse. "It's warm, but it'll do and besides, your face is as red as a tomato, so come on, sit down and drink a little water, okay?"

I did.

"It pays to carry a decent-size purse," she said and frowned at my empty hands. "That's advice you should definitely take to heart. Do you even own a wallet?"

She was acting so normal that I was able to open the water and drink it. She went back to the organ and started practicing the song she'd been playing again. She only stopped once, to tell me to finish the water, and when she was done she shuffled her music together and stood up. Her knees made a loud cracking sound.

"Used to jog when I was younger," she said. "See what you

have to look forward to? Now, come on, get up, and get you something to eat. I have some leftover soup I need to get rid of."

"I—"

"Fine, I'll open a new can just for you." The words sounded like Margaret but her voice was soothing and kind. Understanding.

She called my parents when we got to her house. She didn't ask if it was okay or anything, just told me she was doing it and said I could talk to them if I wanted.

I didn't, so I went into her study and sat on the floor looking at Rose's bears.

"I wanted to let them know where you are," she said when I came back to the kitchen after she'd called that my soup was ready. "They'd like to come pick you up."

"No," I said. It came out louder than I meant it to.

Margaret didn't look surprised, though, just said, "All right. Go wash your hands."

When I came back from the bathroom she was on the phone again. I could tell it was with my parents because I heard her say, "Well, George, I appreciate that," and I went right back into the study and picked up one of the bears. I wondered if Rose's memories were like mine, if she'd seen something like what I had. If she had, how had she ever been able to make anything like this?

Margaret came back when I was still holding the bear and said, "Your parents and I have agreed that I'll drive you home in the morning."

"Oh. Thank—"

Margaret shook her head. "Not necessary." She smiled at the bear, then motioned for me to hand it to her. "Rose was happiest when she was making them, you know. I think they took her away from everything."

"What do you do about your memories?"

Margaret sighed and stroked the top of the bear's head as she put it away. "Think about Rose. Pray. Go talk to Dr. Lincoln, who I've mentioned to you and your parents before. He really is a nice man, Meggie. Terrible posture, but you know how tall people slouch. You should go see him."

"And do what?"

"Talk to him, I would think," she said, squinting at me. "Now come on, your soup is getting cold."

So I ate soup with her and then sat on her sofa while she made more phone calls. She knew a lot of people, and they must have all been old like her because she talked a lot about arthritis and the weather. She usually mentioned Vietnam too, and sometimes she'd say, "Yes, Rose would have liked that."

After every call she'd ask me how I was feeling. I always said I was fine. After her fifth phone call, she sat next to me on the sofa and started eating a candy bar. When she broke off part and held it out to me, I ate it.

"You know what the worst thing about bad days is?" she said. "People try to cheer you up by saying tomorrow is another day or worse, a fresh start. I suppose everyone wants to think that something better must be coming."

I nodded. "Or no one wants to say, 'Sorry, your day sucks but you've still got to get through it.'"

She smiled and handed me another piece of candy bar. "You will get through today, Megan."

"Why? Because I'm a miracle, the girl who survived Flight 619?"

Margaret sighed. "No. I mean you'll get through it because it's after eight already and there's not much of today left. Now, I have to go call my friend Bill and I'll be a while, especially if he starts talking about his back."

He did, and when she finally got off the phone she yawned and then got me a blanket and pillows for the sofa. "Your father told me you like to run at night. He doesn't seem too fond of it. I'm guessing you like it, though?"

I nodded.

She patted the pillows. "It makes you feel better?"

I nodded again.

"You'll stay in town and won't go near strange cars?"

When I looked at her she said, "People do pass through here from time to time, you know. And don't answer me with another nod."

"I don't leave town and I won't talk to strangers. I just—I just like to run."

"Fair enough, but if you track dirt into the house, you have to clean it." She handed me a house key. "This was Rose's. Don't lose it."

"Thank you," I said, and she waved one hand at me and went to bed. I sat on the sofa for a long time and then I got up and went outside. I didn't run. I just sat on her porch. I was careful not to think about anything. I just stared straight ahead, into the dark.

A huge white car drove by when it was so late even the crickets chirping in the grass had gone quiet. It looked like one of Mrs. Harrison's cars. She lived in a huge, old house beside Reardon Logging and made a ton of money renting out rooms to people who worked there and couldn't afford a place of their own. She wore the same three dresses over and over again, and supposedly never did anything to the house, but once a year she'd have someone take her to Derrytown and come back with a big new white car. Then she'd sell her old one. There were about six of them in town now, and they were always easy to spot.

The car slowed down, and Joe's voice called out the window, "Hey, Meggie."

"What are you doing with one of Mrs. Harrison's cars?"

"Bought it from her. Figured since I was already paying her rent and needed a car . . ."

"You're living there?"

"Yeah. I think this thing is bigger than the room she's got me in. It's like driving a boat." He laughed. When I didn't, he turned the car off and got out. "What are you doing here?"

"I—some stuff happened at home. I have to go back in the morning. Are you going to leave your car in the middle of the street?"

"Who's going to be out driving now? Besides me, of course." He walked across Margaret's yard. I waited for him to ask what happened but instead he sat down next to me and said, "Do you want to go home?"

"No. Yes. I don't know."

He grinned at me. "You could always rent a room at Mrs. Harrison's. You'd get to share a bathroom with six other guys and also listen to her talk about how much her feet hurt whenever you pass her on the stairs."

"Do you—do you miss living at home?"

He was silent for a second. "When Beth was alive, I just wanted to get out of there. But after she died and everything fell apart, I missed it. Missed her, missed my parents, missed everything even though things were never all that good. And now I can't even go there anymore. So yeah, I miss it. And you know what the worst thing is?"

I shook my head and wrapped my arms around my knees.

"No one can see how sorry I am about Beth, or how much I miss her, or how I'm not the same guy who slept in detention while his sister died. I can say it, but it's not—if people could somehow see it, if there was something in me or on me that showed it then . . . then maybe my mom would want to talk to me or my dad . . . I don't know. It's stupid."

"It's not. I wish I had a scar or something from the crash. Something that would make my parents see I'm not a miracle. That I'm whatever the opposite of a miracle is."

"Why the opposite?"

"Because I didn't even remember the crash until today. I said I did, but I didn't. I knew that meant something was wrong with me, I knew I should remember. But now that I do, it hasn't made things better. I remember everything and what happened . . . I'm not a miracle, and I already knew that. I just—I still feel as bad as I did before. Worse, even. What I saw . . . what happened . . ." I broke off, shuddered.

He was silent for a long time. "Maybe people like us . . . maybe we don't get better," he finally said. "I feel just as bad now as I did the day I came home and saw Beth's bare feet hanging out the door. Maybe you and I have to learn how to live with what we saw. With what we know."

I pressed my hands against the porch, anchoring myself. "Do you really think that's true?"

"It sucks, so I figure it must be. Are you all right?"

I shook my head.

"Me either. Can I—is it okay if I sit with you for a while?"

"Yeah," I said, and so we sat on the porch and looked out into the dark together.

"So why are you out here?" I said when the sky had started to lighten. "Were you . . . did you see me on your way home from a . . . you know. Thing. Or whatever."

"No," he said. "No thing. Or whatever. I'm not seeing any-one right now. I was just driving around."

"You were just driving around in the middle of the night?"

"You go running in the middle of the night."

"That's different."

He laughed and I felt something strange stretch my mouth. I touched one finger to it.

It was a smile.

"How come you're not seeing anyone?"

"I don't know. I guess maybe I've been spending a lot of time hanging out with this person who likes to talk in the middle of the night, and I feel like she gets me. I actually like her more than I've liked anyone in a long time, so . . ."

I looked over at him, shocked, and my heart started pounding fast and hard. But not from fear. From something else, something new.

"You could say something," he muttered, staring at the ground. "Anything, really."

I looked at him and thought about how I used to see him, and how I saw him now. Who I'd thought he was, and who he really was, and said, "I think you're even better looking inside than you are outside and that—well, that's a lot."

"Meggie," he said, almost helplessly, and for the first time in a long time my name sounded sweet to me. His pinkie brushed against mine, and I didn't move my hand away. We stayed where we were, silent, until the sky turned a pale milky pink and he had to go to work. I missed his pinkie resting against mine after he left.

I was still sitting on the porch when Margaret came out, stretched her arms up over her head, and then sat next to me. "Was that Mrs. Harrison's car parked out in the road in the middle of the night?"

I looked over at her. She was frowning at her flowerbeds.

"I need more mulch," she said and then looked at me. "When Joe first came back to town, I'd never seen anybody look as miserable and lonely as he did. He's looked happier lately. Is that because of you?"

I shrugged. She squinted at me, then pushed her glasses up her nose and got up. "Do you want some breakfast before I take you home?"

"Can I sit here for just a little while longer?"

"Sure," she said, and patted my shoulder. "I'll give you a few minutes. Look, Meggie, you're always welcome here, all right?"

"Thanks."

"But next time you're here and Joe comes by, it had better be daytime, and he'd better not walk all over my flowerbeds. Got it?"

I smiled at her. "Got it."

She tried not to smile back, but I saw a grin quirk the edges of her mouth. "Good."

Twenty-Three

When I got home, Mom and Dad were waiting for me. They looked like they wanted to hug me but I hung back until they stepped away. I could hear David up in his room, stomping around getting ready for school. I'd seen him through his window when I'd come up to the house. He'd looked out and saw me, and then turned away.

"Meggie," Mom said. Her lips were trembling. "We're so glad you're home. And we—" She glanced at Dad, then back at me. "We need to talk."

"I have to talk to David first."

"David?" Dad said. "Sweetheart, you can talk to him later. Right now what's important is—"

"This is important to me," I said, and went upstairs. David was coming out of his room.

"Hey," I said.

"Hey." He tried to walk around me.

"Can I talk to you?" I leaned over to block him. He flinched and then tried to hide it, scowling at me.

"I gotta go wait for the stupid bus."

"It'll just take a second."

He tried to push past me.

"Wait." I grabbed the side of his backpack to stop him, hanging on even though I was holding something disturbingly damp and mushy.

"Quit it."

"David—"

"Let go of my backpack!"

"Fine, I'd love to." I dropped my hand, rubbing it against my leg and trying not to think about why it was so sticky. "Look, I just wanted to tell you—"

He pushed me. "I don't care. All Mom and Dad ever talk about now is you. Everything is about you. You get to do whatever you want just because you were in some stupid plane crash."

I wanted to push him back. I moved away so I wouldn't. "People died, David. I—I saw them. That's not stupid."

"But Mom and Dad said you were the only one who lived after the plane crashed."

"They don't know what really happened. I . . . I had trouble remembering for a while."

"Like you forgot?"

"Yeah."

"Oh." He looked at the stairs and then back at me. "How come?"

"I don't know. I just did."

"But now you remember."

I nodded.

"Is that why you ran away last night?"

"I didn't run away."

He smirked.

"Fine, whatever, David. Look, I just wanted to tell you . . . remember what happened in the kitchen? When I—when I hit you? And then that time in the bathroom? I just wanted to say I'm sorry."

He shrugged. "Okay."

"Okay?"

"Yeah, okay. Can I go now? If I miss the bus I won't get to read Robert's sister's diary. She writes these poems about guys. It's really funny."

"Oh. Sure. Bye."

"Bye." He moved past me and started down the stairs.

Halfway down he came back and hugged me. "I'm glad you didn't die, Meggie."

I hugged him back. "Thanks."

"All right, let go. You stink."

I did, laughing for what felt like the first time in ages. He grinned at me and then ran downstairs. I waited until I heard the front door slam, and then I went to talk to my parents.

I knew I had to do this, that I had to stop pretending for them. I needed to know why they needed me to be fine, to be a miracle, but it was hard to walk toward them.

I was angry—angry and scared and still full of everything that had happened. Everything that I'd remembered. And part of me wished I could forget it all, erase the memories that had returned. The horrible things I'd seen.

Carl was sitting at the bottom of the stairs. He wasn't looking at me. He was staring at his pictures of his wife, his family.

"I'm sorry," I whispered, but he didn't hear me. He couldn't.

Mom and Dad could, though. I took a deep breath and went into the living room where they were waiting for me.

They both stood up when I came in, like I was a guest, and the love and hope and fear on their faces rattled me. I backed up a step, leaning against the door, and they sat down.

"Plenty of space here," Dad said, patting the area between him and Mom on the sofa.

I sat on the floor. Dad's face fell but I didn't move, just waited for him to speak.

He didn't, but Mom did.

"Yesterday, you said some things to me," she said. "You didn't—Meggie, you didn't remember the crash?"

I nodded.

"But in the hospital you said—"

"I wanted to go home. I wanted . . . I wanted you to be happy. To stop looking at me."

"Looking at you?" Dad said.

"You were—you just stared at me. All the time, that's what you did, and I just wanted you stop. I thought if I said I remembered and we went home . . . I thought that at home, everything would go back to normal. That I would. That you would."

"But we . . ." Dad said, and then trailed off, seeing something in my expression. "All right. We tried too hard at first, Meggie. But we were so glad to have you with us. When we got that phone call and had to drive to Staunton, your mother and I thought you were dead. You can't know what that felt like. And then finding out you were alive—"

"It was a miracle," Mom said, and my stomach twisted,

my throat got tight. "You surviving was a—why do you look so upset?"

"You know why," I said, my voice quiet. Broke. "I told you. I'm not a miracle."

"But you lived—"

"Yeah, I lived. But there's something wrong with me and you and Dad know it. I don't sleep. I can't handle going to school. I'm afraid of trees and I run every night because I can't stand being around myself but can't get away. I walk around and wonder if I'm even alive, but all you do is smile and pretend. Why can't you see that I'm not a miracle at all? Why can't you admit that I—?"

I broke off because I was shaking now, scared.

Waiting.

Dad stared at me. His face was pale and he suddenly looked really old, worn-out and sad and scared.

"Meggie, sweetheart," he said and then stopped, folding his hands together and staring down at them like they knew something he didn't.

"It's my fault," Mom said and looked at me, so much pain on her face and in her voice that I wanted to look away but couldn't. She looked like how I felt, and I watched as she got up and walked over to the window.

"My parents said something to me the day I told them I was pregnant with you," she said. "I've never told anyone but your father this, but they said I'd reap what I'd sown. They said everyone I loved would suffer like I'd made them suffer. I was so scared, but then you were born and you were—you were so beautiful, so perfect, that I knew you were a sign that God forgave me for hurting my parents even though they couldn't."

She gripped the curtains in one hand. "But then the phone rang the day you were supposed to come home from camp and your father answered it. He said your name and I—"

"It was like every light in the world went out," Dad said. "Like we—like we were dead too. With David, we knew he had a chance. We knew we could help him. But with you there was nothing we could do. No chance to save you. And then you were alive, and we swore nothing would ever hurt you again. That you would be safe no matter what. That you would be fine."

He cleared his throat, blinking hard, his eyes wet. "Meggie, Margaret mentioned Dr. Lincoln again last night, and I—I think you should go see him. I think we all should go see him. Would you be willing to do that?"

"I don't know," I said. I didn't know if I could talk about the crash. Just thinking about it was bad enough. "Can't we— isn't this enough? I've told you everything, I've told you how I really feel and that . . . you see that now, right?"

Dad started to nod, but Mom shook her head. "I—I think you need help. I think we all do. I think you've felt alone for a long time and I . . . I think you have been. I don't want that for you and I promise . . ."

She broke off and looked at me like she saw me, just me and not a miracle. "I promise that we will try to be what you need. I promise you won't be alone anymore."

Twenty-Four

Mom kept her promise. She and Dad were trying to really be there for me, really see me, and when they smiled at me now I usually felt like they meant it. I still had trouble sleeping, though, and I still saw Sandra or Henry or Walter or Carl when I looked out my window or walked down a hall at school. But I didn't see them as often as I had before, and when I did, I tried not to wish them away. I tried to just see them and keep going.

I still felt like I wasn't real a lot of the time too, and worried that my body would somehow disappear or that I'd end up somewhere else. End up back in the crash. Dr. Lincoln said that was normal. He taught me things to do when I felt like that. Counting backward by sevens, touching something to ground myself, or paying attention to my breathing. Sometimes it helped. Sometimes it didn't. He said that was normal too.

I told Dr. Lincoln what Margaret said about his posture the last time I saw him and he laughed and said he'd be sure to thank her for the advice when he saw her.

"So when you see her, she doesn't spend all her time trying to get you to consume more dairy products?" I said. "How do you manage that?"

"We're talking about you," he said. "Tell me more about what happened when you saw Sandra at school yesterday."

I saw Dr. Lincoln once a week, and every other week me and Mom and Dad and David went in and talked as a family too. Mostly we talked about what was happening with me and school, or Mom and Dad asked me if I was ready to tell them what had happened when the plane crashed. I wasn't. The worst, though, was when David said he felt like no one cared what he did and read a list of things that had happened to him that no one had noticed.

The family sessions weren't my favorite.

Dr. Lincoln and I talked about the crash a lot. I didn't like doing it, and every time we did I had to keep my eyes closed when Mom or Dad drove me home afterward so I couldn't see the hills or the trees. Dr. Lincoln also said I needed to start telling people what had really happened to me. I said it wasn't the kind of thing you started conversations with.

He said, "Are you kidding me? How many times have you

heard someone talk about being in a car accident or how some relative of theirs died in a gruesome way?"

I understood why he and Margaret got along a little better after that.

I saw her once a week too. I was still doing my independent study project, only now I was doing it for real. My topic was women who'd served in the Vietnam War, and Margaret was my project coordinator. I wasn't going to get credit for it, but I still wanted to do it. The first time we all went to see him, Dr. Lincoln told my parents I needed something to focus on besides what had happened, and it needed to be something I liked. They thought soccer. I said no.

Soccer wasn't what it had been to me before. When I thought about it, I only thought about the crash. The game . . . that was gone for me. So I picked doing my independent study project instead. I'd gotten about twenty pages done, which I thought was pretty good. I'd told Margaret that when I saw her yesterday, hoping it would distract her from the fridge and milk.

It didn't work, and when I was done drinking the glass she'd given me, she said, "Now, last time I was telling you about how the hospitals were set up, but I realized I forgot a few things. Do you have any paper? Good. Do you have any that isn't in a notebook that looks like it fell in a puddle?"

"No."

She sighed and went and got some. "I wish Rose could be here," she said when she sat back down. "She could have told someone besides me her story."

"But you guys traveled and talked about the war all the time."

"I did all the talking," she said. "Rose could get other people to talk, but she never talked about what happened to her to anyone but me. I think—I think she might have talked to you, though. I think she would have known you'd understand." She cleared her throat. "How about some more milk?"

I shook my head. She got me a glass anyway.

As I was leaving she said, "I saw Ron Reynolds the other day. He's heading out of town again."

I shrugged.

"I heard he's selling the house."

"He is," I said. "Or at least he's trying to. No one's come to look at it yet."

"And Joe? How's he doing?"

"He's okay," I said. She patted my arm and told me she'd see me soon.

I was pretty sure Joe was okay. He'd found out about the house when he'd come over last Monday. His father had been out front talking to the real estate agent, and he looked surprised when he saw Joe get out of Mrs. Harrison's old car and walk up our driveway. He didn't say anything to him though, and when Joe went over there later he didn't stay long. He called me when he got back to Mrs. Harrison's and told me his dad was selling the house.

"He is?" I said. "Why?"

"He doesn't want to be here anymore."

"What did you say?"

"What could I say? I asked him if I could go to Beth's room. He said no and I went anyway. I have her favorite slippers. I don't know why I grabbed them. I guess I just hate to think of someone buying the house and throwing all her stuff away."

When he came over the next night, I saw he had a black eye. I got him some ice even though he pointed out it wouldn't do any good, and we sat on the porch and talked. He said he wasn't mad at his father.

"I am," I said, and he shot me a quick smile, then looked at the ground.

"I didn't hit him back," he said. "I don't want you to think that I'm like . . ."

"I know who you are," I said, and he looked up and smiled at me again.

My parents had freaked less than I thought they would about us hanging out. He came by to see me the day after I'd had the big talk with them because he hadn't seen me out running. He came by during dinner, which Mom and Dad really didn't like, but they'd only said, "Five minutes," and then peered through the window as we talked out on the driveway. I could tell they thought he wouldn't come back.

He did.

He came by every night and tonight he said he was thinking about getting a dog. He'd have to move out on his own if he did that, though, and he wasn't sure he had enough money or if he wanted to live alone.

"You wouldn't be alone, though. You know that, right?" I looked at the lawn when I said that.

"I know," he said, and we sat with our hands touching until Dad flipped the porch light off and on a bunch of times.

"Subtle," he said, smiling. "I—I called my mom last night. She said she doesn't want to see me. That she can't."

"I'm sorry."

"Yeah," he said, and looked over at his house. "She said that too."

I leaned over and rested my head on his shoulder. "Come over early on Friday, okay? My dad and David are going to Clark when David gets out of school so David can go to the dentist. They'll bring a lot of pizza home."

"Right. I'm sure your parents want me to come over and mooch pizza."

"I want you to."

"Yeah?"

"Yeah."

"Okay then," he said, and squeezed my hand gently. "I will."

I told Mom and Dad about Friday this morning. They looked at each other and then at me.

"You have to stay in the kitchen with us," Mom said.

"At all times," Dad added.

"But he can come?"

They nodded, and then told me to get ready for school. David smirked at me as I grabbed my bookbag. Today was actually a teacher workday. I still had to go to school anyway.

My guidance counselor hadn't come out and said it, but my chances of repeating my senior year were pretty good unless I did a lot of work. We didn't even talk about college. That chance was pretty much gone, especially since I'd officially given up soccer. I told Coach Henson I wasn't ever coming back because Dr. Lincoln said I should. He said it would provide closure.

When I told him, Coach stared at me for a moment before saying, "I already figured that one out, Meggie."

Sometimes Dr. Lincoln didn't know as much as he thought he did.

The plan my guidance counselor and I came up with meant I had a full day of school again, and a lot of homework every night. I had two years of French already, which was what the state required for graduation, and so I was allowed to drop that and spend the class period in the guidance office catching up on homework. I also spent lunch in there doing homework. And at night and on the weekends, when I'd done all my regular homework, I got to do extra assignments to make up for all the ones I'd missed.

My parents were really excited when I first started making up all my work, because they thought it meant something bigger than it was. They thought it meant I was thinking about the future, that I was making plans. I had to tell them to stop. I had to explain that I could still barely deal with my present.

I got to school and took four tests in the guidance office. They were all essay, designed to replace ones I should have taken before. My right hand was numb by the time I was finished.

As I left, I saw Jess and Lissa. They were in the cafeteria with a bunch of people, eating pizza and decorating for a dance. I'd seen posters for it around school. Last year, the three of us had sworn we'd go to every dance together, no dates, just us having fun no matter what our boy situation was.

I'd tried talking to Jess and Lissa right after I started seeing Dr. Lincoln but as soon as I walked up to them in the hall and said, "Hi," I saw Carl standing behind them, cracking his knuckles. I saw myself kneeling next to him while he stared sightlessly at a burning sky. I walked away, hid in the bathroom trying to breathe like Dr. Lincoln said I should, and when I finally went back out into the hall they were gone.

I wouldn't have waited for me either.

When I walked by them as they were decorating for the dance, my hand still smarting from all that writing, Lissa pretended she didn't see me. Jess smiled at me a little though, so I waved. Neither of them waved back.

But they didn't look away either.

When I got home my hand hurt less. My heart did too.

Mom told me to strip my bed so she could wash the sheets. David was out in the backyard doing something with his bike. He waved when I stuck my head out the back door and yelled, "Hey," at him.

Upstairs, I pulled the sheets off my bed and looked out the window. It was going to snow sometime in the next couple of days. I could tell from the sky. It had a kind of heaviness to it, a sense of stillness. Of waiting.

Soon the crash site would be gone, buried under snow, and the spring thaw would wash anything left away.

I wanted to see it. I knew what it looked like in my dreams. In my memories. But now I wanted to see it for real. I needed to.

I went downstairs and found Mom. She'd made David come inside, and they were watching a movie together. He had a new Band-Aid on his hand.

"I have to go out for a while," I told her.

She shook her head. "I don't think so. Where are your sheets?"

"Upstairs. Look, Mom, I want to see where the plane . . . where it crashed."

She looked at me. "David, go upstairs and do your homework."

"I don't have any."

"Then read a book."

"Mom!"

"Go. Now."

He went, and she and I looked at each other.

"Why now?" she said.

"It's going to snow in a few days."

"So?"

"It won't—it won't be there anymore."

"It will."

"Not like it is now. You know what the spring thaw does."

She sighed. "You could get lost."

"I won't. You can call over to the Park Service office and see if they have someone who will take me up there."

"I'll come with you. Let me just call around and see if one of David's friends . . ." She trailed off, frowning at the look on my face. "You don't want me to come with you, do you?"

"It's not—it's not you, not like that. I have to see it the way I saw it when it happened."

"I wish you'd let me come."

"Mom—"

She held up a hand. "I understand what you're saying, Meggie. I do. I just—I wish you'd let me in more."

"I asked," I said. "And I—I've told you why I need to do this. Doesn't that count for something?"

She sighed. "Go get your sheets and put them in the washing machine. I'll call the Park Service office, but if they won't go up with you and won't call me the second you get back, then you can't go."

There was someone at the Park Service office who could drive me up to near the crash site. They were willing to call her after too. When I went outside she came after me, stopping me with a hand on my arm.

"Meggie, please," she said, and then took a deep breath, letting it out slowly. "Please be safe."

I kissed her cheek and got in my car.

Twenty-Five

The person Mom had talked to was waiting for me outside the Park Service office. Her name was Wanda. She was older than Mom, and had long brown hair threaded with gray and a big nose. She knew who I was, and not just because Mom had called her.

"I went out with the team when your plane went down," she said as we shook hands. "Nice to finally meet you. Wish I'd been in town the day you got home."

I mumbled something and thought about going home. I'd had to leave town to get out here though, drove out onto the road that circled Reardon and up into the hills, past endless trees. It had been hard, a lot harder than I thought it would be.

"Come on," Wanda said, jerking her thumb in the direction of a beat-up truck, the Park Service logo barely visible. "We've got a ways to go."

My legs felt like rubber as I walked to the truck, but I did it. I got in. I buckled my seat belt.

"Okay?" Wanda said.

"Okay," I said, and we left.

Wanda didn't talk much as we drove, but after a while she said, "I actually knew Sandra. She'd only been out here a few months. Lived over in Clark because she thought Reardon was too small. I told her that come winter, when she was trying to get out here every morning she'd change her mind. Her husband came out here about a month ago. Brought the baby with him. He wanted to go up to the site too."

"Oh." I hadn't thought about other people wanting to see it. I hadn't thought about the people who'd been left behind, Carl's family and Sandra's and Walter's and Henry's. All those people who'd gotten phone calls like my parents had, only they hadn't had anyone come home.

Stop, I wanted to say, *please stop,* but then she started telling me things I didn't know about all the people that had been with me, that I'd seen too much of and hadn't known at all. She told me she hadn't met Walter, but that there'd been a desk set up for him in the office that he'd never gotten to see. She knew Henry a little, because sometimes he'd come in to talk when the weather was bad enough to ground his plane. She didn't know Carl at all, though she met his wife when she'd come to see the crash site too. She paused then, like she thought I might ask about her, but I couldn't think of a thing to say. "I'm sorry" was too small, too nothing.

We stopped in a stretch of woods that looked like everything else we'd passed.

"We're actually off park land right now and back in Clark County," she said. "Sometimes developers would come through here and talk but since the crash there hasn't been a . . . well." She cleared her throat. "The site's just up over that little hill there."

"It's here?" It couldn't be. I didn't remember this at all.

She nodded. "I'll wait here for you, give you some time alone. Yell if you need anything, though. I'll leave the window down a bit."

I looked out the truck window. Nothing looked familiar. Maybe I'd remembered things wrong. What if I had? My palms were sweating. Maybe I should just ask to go back. Maybe this was a really bad idea. Maybe . . .

Maybe I needed to do this. Maybe if I walked up to where she'd told me the site was, I'd know it. Maybe then it would all make sense. Maybe then I'd finally know why it happened. Why I'd lived.

I got out of the truck.

I walked up the hill. The wind blew, the trees rustled, and the ground was uneven, rocky. But it still didn't look familiar.

Then I reached the top of the hill.

It was there. The rocks, the ground, the trees I'd fled into, terrified of looking back. It was all there.

But it wasn't like I remembered.

I remembered an endless expanse of torn, burning ground. I remembered fire and debris and death. It wasn't like that. There was a small clearing, a patch of dirt and stubborn rock that had shoved its way up out of the ground and pushed back the trees. There were black marks on some of the rocks, dark like they had been burned. I knew that was from the plane.

I knew this place.

I had to sit down then. I covered my face with my hands and closed my eyes. This was it. I'd been here. A part of me would always be here.

After a while, the wind blew again, and I heard a sound I knew too well. I opened my eyes and looked at the trees. They were smaller than I remembered, and sparser. Some of them had been burnt, leaving behind only withered black skeletons. The fire had done that. It must have happened after I'd gone. I only remembered stumbling toward greenness, being swallowed by it. I remembered being afraid to look back, afraid I'd see what I so wanted to forget.

I looked around the clearing. The ground was rubbed

raw in a few places, scrubbed by fire, but otherwise it looked untouched. I knew it had been, though.

Someone had left a wreath of flowers on top of the tallest rock. They looked brittle in the wind, dried out and rustling. I didn't want to look at them. I didn't want to see who had left them.

I looked around again. I knew that corner, over by those rocks. I'd seen Walter there. I'd watched his hat drift away. And there, on the other side, that was where Sandra—I bent down, pressed both hands into the ground. The dirt was cold and rocky, scraped my fingers.

The last time I'd felt it, it had been wet and hot, searing my skin.

I looked behind me. There was a faint groove cut into the ground, and I knew that once it had been deeper. That I'd crawled out of a piece of the plane by it, Carl's hand clasped in mine.

I didn't cry. The pain inside me was too raw for tears. This was where I'd closed my eyes and woke up to a burning sky.

I didn't want to see it again, but I looked up anyway.

The sky wasn't burning. It was cloudless and blue, the gentle color of late afternoon. It was now. It was real.

I got up and walked away.

Wanda didn't ask me how it went when I got back to her. She didn't say anything at all. Maybe she could tell I didn't want to talk. Maybe she was tired. I was grateful for the silence as we drove back, and watched the forest growing dark around us. I didn't like seeing the trees.

I looked at them anyway.

Once Joe said that maybe people like us couldn't get better, that maybe we had to learn to live with what we'd seen. What we knew.

When we got back, I asked Wanda to hold off calling my house for a little while.

"I don't know," she said. "I promised I'd call right away, and it's getting awful dark out. I couldn't let you go back up into the hills by yourself now."

"I don't want to do that, I promise. I just need to go see someone in town real fast."

She looked at me and then sighed. "Well, I guess I could wait a little while."

"Thanks."

She nodded. "I get needing a little time. The team I was with . . . we were the first ones there. We all looked at—well, we all looked around and were sure no one could have lived through that. But you did, didn't you?"

"I did," I said, and for the first time the fact that I'd lived didn't feel like something I'd never understand. It just felt like something that was.

When I drove away, Wanda waved goodbye, and in the rearview mirror her arm swayed like a tree in the wind. I waved back, and watched until she disappeared.

Joe's car wasn't parked by Mrs. Harrison's house. It was by the town cemetery near Reardon Logging, up by where the hills began. I drove past it, then turned around and went back. It took me a little while to get out of the car.

Beth's grave was toward the back, by the sharp swell of earth that marked the true beginning of the hills. Joe was sitting cross-legged on the ground next to a stone that had her name carved across it.

"Hey," I said when I reached him.

He looked up at me, surprised. "What are you doing here?"

"I saw your car out front. Don't you usually come here later?"

"Yeah, but sometimes there's stuff I really want to tell her. Like today I . . . here, let me move over so you can sit down too."

I did, folding my legs like his. "Thanks. So, today you told her what?"

"Just stuff."

I looked at him.

"I was . . . all right, don't laugh, okay? I was telling her about Friday."

"Why would I laugh? I'm glad you said you'd come."

We glanced at each other, and then looked away.

"I'm kinda glad you weren't here about five minutes ago, actually. I was practicing stuff to say to your parents." He grinned at me, and then tilted his head a little to one side. "You okay?"

I looked down at the ground. "I went up into the hills this afternoon."

"Oh. To see—"

"Yeah. Where the plane crashed."

"Have you been there since—?"

"No," I said. I wanted to say more, but I couldn't. He didn't say anything either.

After a while, I looked over at him. He was looking at me. "Do you want to be alone for a while?"

"I don't know," I said.

He was silent for a second, and then said, "I'll go. It's a good place to think about . . . stuff."

I looked at Beth's grave, all Joe had left of his family. I read her name again, and then looked up into the hills. "You can stay if you want."

"You sure?"

I nodded and looked away from the hills. I looked at the

sky. It was clear and dark, speckled with stars. It was beautiful. It was real.

I was real.

I looked at Joe. I took a deep breath.

"When I woke up," I said, "the sky was burning."

Author's Note

I don't like writing about having PTSD. I feel a constant need to apologize for having it because I haven't been in combat or the victim of a violent crime. My therapist says this is a huge part of why I refused to see what was happening for so long.

I suspect she's right.

In 2003, about a week after I'd gone from being the only allergy-free person in my immediate family to the one with more allergies than all of them combined, I had my first run-in with anaphylaxis.

The culprit?

Food.

For a few days after my trip to the ER, I would make myself something to eat, but within a few bites, I'd have to stop because I was sweating and shaking and convinced I could feel an itch forming in my throat.

Then I realized if I didn't eat, I'd be totally safe, because if I didn't eat, I wouldn't die.

So I stopped eating.

I woke up two days later in the middle of the night,

sweating and screaming. I passed out trying to get up. My husband and parents (who'd come up while I was in the ER) forced me to eat two tablespoons of sugar, and the next morning I found myself headed toward my parents' home, where I spent the next six weeks learning to eat again.

It was hell. I wept the first time I ate a bite of chicken. I curled up in a ball on the floor for an hour after eating half a cup of rice. I was so sure I was going to die, but as the weeks went by, I gradually realized I wouldn't die if I ate foods I wasn't allergic to.

I ate a very restricted diet for three years after that, and eventually managed to get into the high double digits of things I would eat without fear. I learned to act like I didn't care that I was allergic to so many things, and it didn't take very long for me to believe it.

It wasn't until I started seeing a therapist in 2011 that I realized I wasn't okay with what had happened. In fact, when I decided to have full allergy testing done again in early 2012 and found myself having nightmares, I kept wondering why I was so scared. I'd had the testing before. It took a while, sure, but it wasn't painful.

My therapist told me that I wasn't afraid of the testing, but that I was very afraid of what might happen afterward because of what had happened before. And after she asked me to talk about what had happened, she showed me a check-list for PTSD symptoms and I found out—nearly nine years later—that I have PTSD.

I'm not nearly as aware or as brave as Megan is, but I've come to see that when I wrote *Miracle*, it was my subconscious screaming at me to see what was going on inside me. I've always sworn I'd never write about myself or anyone I know, but it turns out that *Miracle* is the most personal thing I've ever written. It just took me a long time to realize it.

If you or anyone you know has undergone a traumatic experience of any kind, please visit http://www.nimh.nih.gov/health/publications/post-traumatic-stress-disorder-ptsd/what-are-the-symptoms-of-ptsd.shtml to learn more and make sure you get the help you need.

About the Author

Elizabeth Scott is also the author of *Bloom*; *Perfect You*; *Living Dead Girl*; *Something, Maybe*; *The Unwritten Rule*; and *Between Here and Forever*. She lives just outside Washington, D.C., with her husband, firmly believes you can never own too many books, and would love it if you visited her website (elizabethwrites.com), followed her on Twitter (twitter.com/escottwrites), and became a fan on Facebook (facebook.com/elizabethwrites).

bloom

ELIZABETH SCOTT

"A fresh, honest,
and heartfelt story
of first love."
—DEB CALETTI
National Book Award finalist for
Honey, Baby, Sweetheart

ON PAPER, LAUREN'S LIFE IS PERFECT: GOOD GRADES,
nice friends, amazing boyfriend. So why is she so unhappy?
And what does the new boy in school have to do with it?

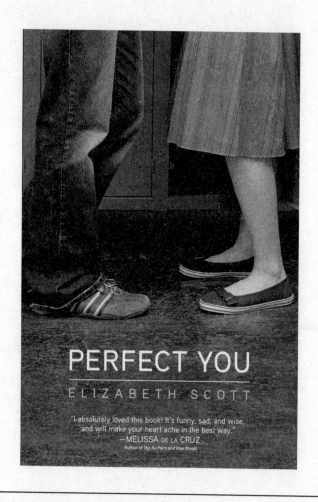

PERFECT YOU

ELIZABETH SCOTT

"I absolutely loved this book! It's funny, sad, and wise,
and will make your heart ache in the best way."
—MELISSA DE LA CRUZ
Author of *The Au Pairs* and *Blue Bloods*

KATE'S LIFE HAS TAKEN A TURN FOR THE WORSE.
Her best friend has become popular and acts like Kate's invisible,
and Kate has to work for her dad selling vitamins at the mall. The
one bright spot is Will, the guy she can't stop thinking about. . . .
Too bad he's also the guy most likely to break her heart.

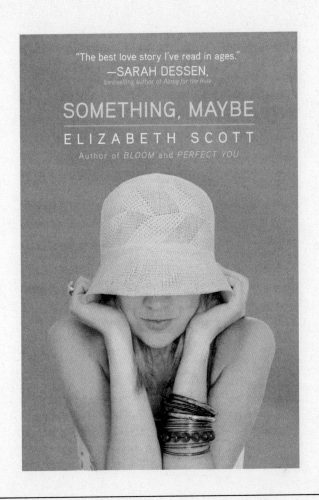

"The best love story I've read in ages."
—SARAH DESSEN,
bestselling author of *Along for the Ride*

SOMETHING, MAYBE

ELIZABETH SCOTT

Author of *BLOOM* and *PERFECT YOU*

HANNAH HAS MASTERED THE ART OF STAYING under the radar, but that means her crush doesn't know she's alive. Is that why her goofy friend Finn seems so appealing, because he's there? Or could it be something more . . . ?

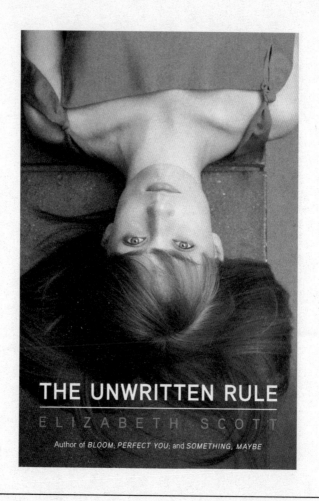

THE UNWRITTEN RULE

ELIZABETH SCOTT

Author of *BLOOM*; *PERFECT YOU*; and *SOMETHING, MAYBE*

SARAH HAS LIKED RYAN FOR FOREVER, BUT HE'S dating her best friend. And everyone knows the rule: You don't mess around with your friend's boyfriend. Despite her efforts to avoid Ryan, she can't stop wanting him. And when they are alone together one night, there's no turning back.

BETWEEN HERE AND FOREVER

ELIZABETH SCOTT

Author of *BLOOM* and *PERFECT YOU*

"Compulsively readable . . . will appeal to fans of Sarah Dessen and Gayle Forman."—*SLJ*

ABBY'S SISTER, TESS, IS IN A COMA, AND ABBY'S life is on hold. When Abby learns a shocking secret about Tess—something that was always right there, but she'd never seen—she must come to terms with the fact that Tess may not have led the picture-perfect life after all.

living

dead

girl

A NOVEL

"Stark. Gripping. Totally unforgettable."
—Ellen Hopkins, author of *CRANK*

ELIZABETH SCOTT

ALICE WAS KIDNAPPED BY RAY FIVE YEARS AGO.
She has learned to endure the pain and waits for the night-
mare to be over. Ray speaks more and more of her death, but
she does not yet realize he has something even more terrifying in mind for her.

Rebecca Serle

when you were mine

WHAT IF THE GREATEST LOVE STORY EVER
TOLD WAS THE WRONG ONE?

EBOOK EDITION ALSO AVAILABLE

WHAT IF THE GREATEST LOVE STORY EVER TOLD WAS THE WRONG ONE?

"Romeo didn't belong with Juliet; he belonged with me.
It was supposed to be us together forever, and it would have been
if she hadn't come along and stolen him away. Maybe then all of
this could have been avoided. Maybe then they'd still be alive."

From Simon Pulse | TEEN.SimonandSchuster.com | rebeccaserle.com

THREE HEARTBREAKING AND GUT-WRENCHING STORIES ABOUT FRIENDSHIP, LOVE, AND LOSS

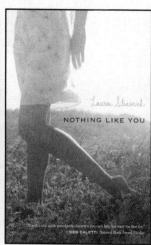

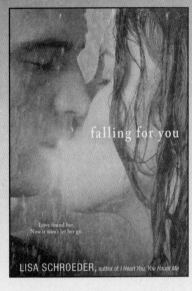

SimonTEEN

Simon & Schuster's **Simon Teen**
e-newsletter delivers current updates on
the hottest titles, exciting sweepstakes, and
exclusive content from your favorite authors.

Visit **TEEN.SimonandSchuster.com** to
sign up, post your thoughts, and find out what
every avid reader is talking about!

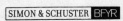